SEVEN FOR THE SEA

SEVEN FOR THE SEA

W. Towrie Cutt

FOLLETT PUBLISHING COMPANY
Chicago

ISBN 0-695-40480-6 Titan binding
ISBN 0-695-80480-4 Trade binding

Library of Congress Catalog Card Number: 73-93556

First Printing

TO MARGARET NANCY

The author wishes to acknowledge his debt to
Madeau Stewart for her work in editing the book and
selecting the illustrations.

CONTENTS

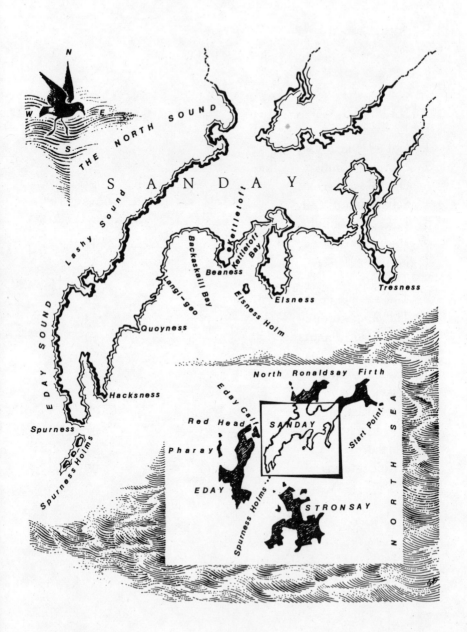

Chapter 1

OUT OF THE FOG

IN THE THICK FOG that shrouded Kirkwall Harbor the steve-
dores and sailors worked sullenly as they loaded the last of
the cargo aboard the *Sigurd*. On deck in the cold, damp
air, two boys, Mansie Ward and his cousin Erchie, looked
glumly into the swirling murk.

Mansie had come in to the harbor from his home on
the Orkney island of Sanday, off the northeastern coast of
Scotland, to meet his cousin Erchie from Edinburgh. On
this, the first day of their holiday and the longest day of
the year, both boys had looked forward to good weather.

"I long for the boat to be off," said Erchie, "and to be
with Uncle George, Aunt Jessie, and Peter tonight."

A few late passengers tramped dejectedly up the
gangway which the sailors now prepared to haul away.

"Look at that Shetland collie, Mansie!"

Mansie looked to see a dog being lifted from the quay
down to a sailor who took him and led him away.

"Boy! A beauty of a dog, but the poor thing's frightened. I wonder why?"

Just then the captain blew the warning whistle, the
sailors made all snug, and soon the *Sigurd* was steaming

9

slowly into the fog. Sunlight brightened up the gray ahead, and the ship began to move faster through a radiant and thinning mist. The boys began to feel more cheerful.

"The Selkie Wards!" exclaimed Erchie suddenly. "Mansie, is it true that our great-grandmother was a sea maiden?"

"That's an old wife's tale, Erch! But our great-great-grandmother and six of her sons were lost at sea in a storm. The boat was found, but no bodies, and folks said she had gone back to the sea."

"Oh," exclaimed Erchie, "then perhaps *she* was the sea maiden. And it must have been our great-great-grandfather who was nicknamed Selkie. Why was that?"

"My father told me that Selkie Ward was like my brother Peter, always wandering about the shore by himself and speaking to the seals—the selkies."

"And my father told me," said Erchie, "that Selkie Ward wore a sealskin vest—wore it against his skin like a hair shirt, for something bad he had done."

"Peter has that vest now, but I never heard of it being worn like a hair shirt. It's handed down from Peter Ward to Peter Ward—from seventh son to seventh son. And every seventh son is called Peter. Seven is a magical number. I don't know why."

"I do want to see your brother Peter again!" said Erchie. "Remember him down on the ebb last year, when he was speaking to the two seals—only you thought they were kelpies."

"They had heads like horses, Erch. They were kelpies."

"I didn't notice the heads. How long will it take us to reach Sanday now, Mansie?"

"Another five hours or more."

The mist continued to clear, and after a while Erchie began to hope that they would see the familiar village of Kettletoft and Elsness Holm which was a small island in the distance. The *Sigurd* was now approaching Green Holms, a group of small islands. "The gray seals have their pups in there, Erchie," said Mansie, pointing, "but we'll no see them in the haze."

"Many seals?"

"Hundreds."

The sudden cutting off of the engine made the boys go to the side of the steamer and look over. A yawl from the island of Eday was coming alongside. Two women passengers came on deck, looked in disgust at the mist, and then nervously at the yawl. They were assisted down into it, some mail sacks were lowered after them, and the yawl then bore away. As the *Sigurd* moved off, the air started to darken again and the boys' spirits sank.

"Don't lean so far oot, Mansie boy," said an old sailor as he passed. "If that black wall clears of a sudden there'll be nothing to stop you falling head first into the sea!"

The two lads drew back and then forced a laugh.

"The ship's turned a little," said Mansie after a while, "so we must be clear into Sanday Sound."

"Then we should be at the pier in half an hour or less."

"We might. The Captain's going slow, though he knows the way. He'll never see the pier in this fog."

"Aunt Jessie will worry about us."

"Oh, Mother will not think about it. She's used to it."

The dark wall of fog still imprisoned the *Sigurd* as she edged forward. Minutes dragged past—endless minutes they seemed to the boys. Then came a shout from the sailor at the bow: "Two fathoms!" He had been taking soundings. The engine stopped, and the ship heaved gently.

"Ahoy, *Sigurd!*"

A hollow call came from the port side. The engine started slow ahead. "All right to come in?" shouted the Captain through a horn.

The voice came faintly. "I doubt if ye can get a line ashore. Can't see me hand afore me face."

"I'll anchor and wait for it to clear," shouted the Captain.

"That's a blessing," came back in ghostly tones.

The anchor chain rattled out. A few passengers who had come on deck when the engine stopped returned sourly to the cabin. All the sailors, with the exception of the lookout man who remained at his post in the bow went to the upper deck. The boys wandered about in the middle section of the ship, searching into the darkness that hid the pier and the village where the Ward family—Jessie, George, and Peter—must be waiting for them. They stopped now by the Shetland collie. Stretched out on the cold deck, its nose to the boards, it looked up at them with its soft brown eyes.

"Oh, collie," exclaimed Erchie. "Tied here with nobody you know."

"That's the way the selkies look up at you, Erch."

The boys stroked the collie, and he stood up, nosed at their legs, and wagged his tail.

"I don't like it," muttered Mansie as he peered into the fog.

"It's a nuisance," agreed Erchie, "but we're safe enough here till it clears."

"Safe enough! In a steamer in the middle of the day and it could be the middle of the night. And this the longest day of the year—Johnsmas. Anything can happen on Johnsmas when the tide's nearly full and the moon as well. I don't like it."

Erchie knelt down by the collie, and Mansie sat beside him—then suddenly got up again. Once more he peered into the fog and drew his breath in sharply.

"What was that, Mansie?"

"It was two . . . Quiet, Erch! A boat," breathed Mansie, and they both listened to the dull dip of oars which sounded as though they were muffled. The faint drip that followed each muted splash told them that the boat was at hand. Then a coal-black shape loomed on the darkness of the water.

"Anyone want ashore?" came from the boat in a ghostly, droning voice.

"Aye," answered Mansie readily. He ran down the companionway and seized the end of a line tied to a pin.

"But Mansie," whispered Erchie, following.

"We'll get our suitcases later when the ship comes in," said Mansie. He was now up on the gunwhale and then lowered himself down over the side, while Erchie held his breath. "But Mansie . . ." he whispered urgently again.

"Come on, Erch," called Mansie impatiently.

Erchie gripped the rope and lowered himself down. He had hardly dropped into the boat when the boatman pulled away. The two boys wobbled, and sat down breathless on the stern timbers, there being no floor boards. The boatman, a black blur, seemed to pull on invisible oars. A piteous wail from the collie on the *Sigurd* followed them, like a cry for help.

The boatman was as silent as the fog itself, but his oars kept up a steady rhythm. Pressed together in the stern, the boys strained to see him better. Mansie ran his fingers along the timbers and found that they were covered in black tar.

Erchie gasped, "Mansie, I saw two seal things with heads like horses. . ."

"Aye, the kelpies. I saw them too from the ship. Was that what you wanted to tell me as we left?"

"Yes. Aren't they wicked fairies of a kind? Don't they lead sailors to their doom, Mansie?"

"Ach! Likely pirates said that to explain away the ships they sank. I like the kelpies. When I saw them, I decided to get into the boat. They know their way, even in a fog."

Misgivings filled Erchie as he heard this; Mansie must be in one of his strange moods again. But Mansie looked at him with a grin. "Look, Erch! There's sand on the bottom. We must be close in, and this is the channel to Towrie's Green."

"That's very near your house, isn't it?"

"Aye." At that moment the boat grounded at the bow.

The fog had lifted, and the small green appeared in bright sunshine.

"Henry!" shouted Mansie.

The boatman did not answer. He put his oars into the boat and got out, holding the rope that he used to secure the boat at the dock. The boys followed as he went up on shore.

"How are you keeping, Henry?" asked Erchie.

The little man with the stiff, black beard did not reply at once. Then, in the droning voice of Henry Goar, an

14

old friend of the family, he said, "I don't ken ye lads. Ye're from the south, by your clothes."

"My clothes, Henry?" said Mansie, startled. "Ach, stop thee teasing."

"And thanks for taking us from the steamer, Henry," said Erchie.

"Steamer? Whit steamer?"

"The *Sigurd*. Out there!" said Erchie impatiently.

They looked to the sea. There was no mist now. And there was no *Sigurd*. No ship anywhere.

Chapter 2

FROM WINDMILL
TO WATERMILL

KETTLETOFT BAY, clear under a high sun, lay calm and blue in front of them, but it was empty. The familiar big house and farm buildings of Elsness lay across the bay, and the two Isegarth cottages were in their places at the far end. Seaward, there was the islet Elsness Holm with its little ruined house. But there was no pier and still no *Sigurd.*

In dismay the boys looked from their boatman to the left and to the right. The village they had known, harbor stores, post office buildings, and houses seemed gone with the fog. Only a short row of low buildings with a windmill at one end stood near, and this was in sad repair.

"This *is* Sanday," cried Erchie. "There's Kettletoft Bay, and there's the Elsness Holm. But where's the village? Where's the ship? The pier?"

"Oh, ships come, and ships go," droned the little stiff-bearded boatman.

"Where's Kettletoft village, Henry, and where's my parents' house?" pleaded Mansie.

16

"There's no village here," answered the man, "and never has been. Only that empty hoose there, and it's named Kettletaft. There's never a pier. Just that narrow inlet there through the rocks where the boats tak' ashore the cargo from ships to the store, ye see." He pointed to a large building in good repair less than half a mile away, a building the boys had known as a roofless and crumbled ruin. Even the high old kiln at the land end was complete, a gentle smoke rising from the stack. The boys stared, fear gripping them.

"Henry," asked Erchie timidly, "where's my uncle George Ward?"

"I ken no George Ward. Selkie Ward—his real name's Ollie—lives at Walbreck, if ye're seekin' him."

"Selkie Ward!" exclaimed Erchie. "But he's been dead for a hundred years. He was our great-great-grand-father."

"Weel, weel, have it your own way, but he's living this day, and that I ken. Go over the hill there, and across Beasand, and along the crags to Walbreck, and you'll find him. Noo, I think you lads should respect your elders, even if ye're from the Sooth, and no spin yarns to the likes o' me. Goodday to ye baith. We'll meet again, maybe."

The little man turned his back on them, and moved off with a stiff-legged gait down to his boat. The sounds he made could either have been mutters or chuckles.

"Henry! Henry! We're not telling you yarns!" cried Mansie.

"Maybe ye're no, and maybe I'm no Henry," he droned as he pushed off the boat, got in, and pulled rapidly away from the beach.

The boys stared after him, and then at each other, and then all around. No ship, no pier, no village. Only a deserted little farm. The boatman was rowing along Beaness, just where the pier and slip should be.

"It can't be," breathed Erchie.

"It's no joke," murmured Mansie. "Johnsmas. And the moon will be full tonight."

"Yes, yes, Johnsmas," echoed Erchie, "and those kelpies. I don't trust them. Now where's Henry?"

"Mercy! Where can he have got to?" Mansie was startled.

"Could he be around Beaness by this time?"

"He was pulling strongly, but I don't think so. We'll go 'round the cape to see if he's there."

As they hurried along a rutted old road past where the pier should have been, Mansie said, "Henry's having fun wi' us I think. He's known me all my life."

"And he must remember me. We spoke to him a lot last year, and he told us he was descended from a Spaniard from an Armada ship wrecked in the Orkneys."

"Aye, and it was he who hinted that we came from a selkie because of the reddish tinge on our necks and the hard skin between our fingers."

"There's no sign of him yet, Mansie, but he may be round the point."

"He must be somewhere," went on Erchie as they rounded the headland and could see into Backaskaill Bay. They looked everywhere, but the bay and shore were empty. "The pier's nowhere, and the village is nowhere. There's only an old house and a windmill that weren't there before. That's what comes of following kelpies. Now what do we do? Where do we go?"

"Walbreck," declared Mansie readily. "Our great-great-grandfather Ward's there—if Henry's right in his head."

"Our great-great-grandfather! Are you right in your head, Mansie! Midsummer madness! Let's go then, if you know the way."

"Walbreck is a field on the hill called Warsetter. There are steethes of old cottages there."

"Foundations you mean? I don't remember seeing them."

"I've seen them often enough." Mansie looked across the fields of the cape. "Where can the new house of Howe be? There's the old house and the barns and the plough-men's houses."

"Where's anything I know?" said Erchie. "Oh, let's go to Selkie Ward if there is such a man."

The boys walked quickly along the shore they knew, noting the animals in the fields of the large farm of Howe, but paying little attention, for their thoughts were on what had happened since they had left the *Sigurd*. They came to the sluice that released the water in the old days. Water was pouring through it. Looking up along the mill dam, as the ditch through which the water ran was called, they saw the big wheel turning. When they listened, they heard a grinding, shaking noise from the mill.

"The mill is working," said Erchie.

"We'll go up along the dam, Erch. Maybe I'll see somebody I know."

"But we both knew Henry who is not the Henry we knew."

"Aye, but everybody won't be like that—I hope. Come on."

As they approached the mill, the noise increased. They looked up to a high window on the third floor. A man was leaning out. He had a mealy cap pulled down over his eyes, and he turned his head first one way and then another, watching. He drew in as he saw the boys, then shut the window and disappeared.

The big water wheel looked new to the lads, and yet last year they had seen it old and decaying. They stood watching, fascinated by the water pouring down from the rising cross-pieces. They went on a short distance where they could see water flowing down the lade onto the cross-pieces and weighting them down, thus turning the wheel. The many noises of water and the monotonous grinding and shaking from within almost deafened them. They crossed a little bridge over the dam, and went to the large open door of the mill. A stout man inside was hooking a sack of grain to a hoist. As the sack moved up through a hatch in the ceiling of the first floor, the man turned around.

"Who may ye two lads be?" he asked in a deep, pleasant voice.

"We're Ward boys and goin' to Walbreck," answered Mansie.

"Ye're from the South, I warrant."

"I am," said Erchie, "but . . ."

"Hide it, Jeems. They're comin' doon the Howe road," yelled a voice from above.

"Aye, aye," said the stout man coolly.

"Quick, man! Give the boys the two sacks of chaff and send them off."

"So ye're for Selkie Ward," said the miller slowly. "That's what I thought. Tak' the two sacks o' chaff to him, for he wants them for his bed. There's no weight in them." He held both up in one hand. "Noo, ye'll hurry past the churchyard. The ghosts are slow in the afternoon, but they might come at ye." He slung a sack onto Mansie's back and another onto Erchie's.

"Hurry now, boys, hurry." And the miller himself made haste through a door, leaving the boys dumbfounded.

But remembering their orders, they hurried over the high bank of the dam and were concealed from the road. Bearing their ticklish sacks, they now ran up to and past the churchyard gate, not knowing why they hurried, and then down the dug-out road to Beasand, which stretched flat and wide for half a mile ahead. They came to a little stream flowing over soft sand and crossed it.

"We're safe across running water," laughed Erchie. "That miller still believes in ghosts!"

They stopped, put down their sacks, and scratched their necks. A shout drew their attention, and they quickly picked up their sacks and looked around.

A tall, dark, red-faced man on a shaggy pony galloped towards them.

"Stop in the King's name!" he commanded and dismounted.

"You mean the Queen's—Elizabeth," corrected Erchie. "If not, what king?" He was thinking they might be in a strange land.

"Our Monarch, William the Fourth, is a long time after Elizabeth, who never was queen here, you ignorant young whelp. Put down those sacks," he ordered, in a harsh voice.

The boys obeyed. The man lifted one sack, tested its weight, and shook his head. He untied it and poured the contents out. The chaff made a small dusty cloud that, when it settled, covered the clear water of the little stream with a yellow scum.

"Devil take it," muttered the man, frowning, and he seized the other sack.

"Sir," protested Erchie, "the miller asked us to take these sacks of chaff to Selkie Ward. Now he'll have no chaff for his bed."

The man paid no heed, but emptied the second sack. Again a little cloud of dust and chaff. Again he frowned.

"Old Moodie told you that, did he? The old scamp! He'll have the malt hid by now, but I'll catch the old fox yet. I'm the exciseman, me lads—the gauger that measures the malt to see His Majesty gets his due. Well, I know that Moodie has malt there and too much of it."

"You mean Selkie Ward doesn't want the chaff?" asked Mansie.

"Ho, ho, ho!" laughed the gauger.

"The miller asked if we were from the South," Erchie added.

"Ho, ho, ho. He needn't have asked, and knew he could trick you. The malt must still be in the mill. I'm sure of it."

He mounted his little pony and spurred her back the way he had come.

"What's all this about, Mansie?"

"Long ago the folks brewed a lot of ale and made whisky from malt and it was against the law. They were always in trouble with the exciseman. Father told me stories about them. But that was long before his time."

"I can't understand it. When that man talked of the king, I thought we might be in another country."

"Neither do I understand. But there's a Selkie Ward in Walbreck, that we do know. Let's go on."

"To Selkie Ward and his seal wife?"

"We'll see, Erch, we'll see."

22

Chapter 3

ON TO WALBRECK

THE BOYS WALKED ON. Sand, sea, and cliff were familiar, as was the large farm building of Backaskaill lying in front of them. Looking directly landward to the links, or sand hills, Erchie saw half a dozen horses.

"Look, Mansie. I didn't see a horse here last year."

One horse raised its head from grazing and came into full view from the hollow behind the shore.

"There were four in the island last year," answered Mansie. "These are shaggy little beasts, and the sheep in the next field are small brown things. I don't remember those either."

"What's that line of people up on the hill doing?" asked Erchie, pointing.

Mansie saw a line of people all stooped, and moving slowly over the field. "They must be planting turnips. Probably folks from Backaskaill, for there's nobody around the farm."

After passing the farmhouse, they climbed a path to the cliffs and came upon a circle dug out of the cliff top near a geo, as a small inlet or gully is called. The pit was

23

about five feet across, and was full of dark, grayish substance that had been flattened down.

"That must be the kelp—the ashes of seaweed. They don't burn it today, but ship it in bundles."

They now reached two cottages with attached buildings. The nearest cottage was very low and thatched-roofed. The further cottage was roofed with flag-stones, and had a well-built stone fence in front.

"I think that's Walbreck," said Mansie, pointing to the further one. "We'll go and ask. I heard a rooster crow, so somebody must be living in it."

They went over a rough stone fence into a small field with six ewes and ten lambs lying down in it. These rose, bunched together, and stared at the boys with ears erect, the little brown ewes seeming prepared to charge. But four put their heads down again and lay down with their lambs. The other two slowly came to the boys, each with a lamb, and much to Erchie's delight, one rubbed against him, and the lambs came to be fondled. "Come on, Erch! We can't spend all the day with the ewes," said Mansie.

After climbing over another stone fence which enclosed the cottage and its attached buildings, they saw an old and wrinkled woman down on her knees before the cottage door. She had one hand up, dropping grains, and the other moved clockwise in circles.

"Mighty!" exclaimed Mansie. "She's grinding corn, with stones, poor body."

"I've never seen that done."

"I tried it once, to see how it worked. It didn't work well, and it was a slow job."

The old woman looked up, showing a thin, wizened face with watery blue eyes under a black head shawl. "Were ye two lads wantin' me man?" she asked, and went on, "He's at Warsetter buildin' a wall for the laird." She fingered into a cone of rough paper, brought out some cloves and put them in her mouth.

"No, ma'am. We're looking for Mr. Ward," answered Erchie.

"Ye speak like one from the Sooth."

"I am," said Erchie. "My name is Erchie Ward."

"Oh! Aye," continued the old woman in a firmer voice, "Selkie has relations doon there, but they never come to see him noo. If they did, they'd find him a changed man. Aye, changed altogether."

"How is he changed?" asked Mansie.

"Well, he used to drink hard, and lost nigh all he had. Then one harvest he took a wife to himsel' and he's a changed man."

"That's his house down there, isn't it?" asked Mansie.

"That it is, and as neat and prosperous place as any you'll see. The ground was said to be good for nothing. That's why Selkie got it when he had drunk himself oot o' his father's cottage. Nobody deemed he could mak' a living on it, and he did no until he got her."

"Was she . . . was she one of the neighbors?" inquired Erchie.

"No, he brought her home in his boat one day, but I don't ken what island he got her. All I ken is he did himsel' a good turn."

"She must be a fine woman," said Erchie.

"As good a body as you could get," declared the old woman. "Many a jug o' milk and many an egg has she sent up here by one of her children, and fish when she has them, and that's most o' the time. Me and me man's been failing in our health, ye see." The old woman put more cloves into her mouth. "And she kens I like the cloves, and

25

gets me some whenever she can." She laid down the twist of cloves.

"It's grand folks here like her," said Mansie.

The old woman peered at him. "Mind thee, boy, it's no that many like her. They say she's a witch, and call her all the names their dirty tongues can get aroond."

"A witch?" asked Erchie. "Why? Surely they know there aren't any witches."

The old woman shook her head sadly. "It's little thoo kens aboot folk, boy. I was hounded and so was me man, for long ago we went oot in our old boat and guided a ship that was in trouble into the bay o' Stove. They called me a witch, for the sea was high, but no that bad. They would sooner see dead sailors than miss the drift from a wreck. Aye, me man built hooses once, and noo only fences because o' their clashes and clatters. Seawife has me old boat, noo, for I'm past usin' it."

"Seawife? That's Mrs. Ward, is it? And she does no witch-work," said Erchie.

"She kens the fishing grounds better than any man here. She looks after her lambs and cows so that they thrive. That's the only witch-work she does." The old woman mumbled on her cloves in anger.

"That's Mr. Ward's house, isn't it?" asked Erchie, pointing to the next cottage. "We're going there. Thank you, ma'am."

"Weel-spoken lads like you can be sure o' a welcome. Good-day to ye both."

The two boys returned to the cliff edge. Two fulmars glided and hovered just by their heads. Below, on the rocks a shag perched, and beyond in the sea, a group of eider ducks swam—the brown hen with the black and white drake, and four brown ducklings. The sea was flooding in with a gentle swell towards the green bay. There was nothing strange seaward, except at Beaness where no chimneys and no village roofs could be seen.

A hundred yards from the cliff stood Walbreck, just where the level ground began to rise to the hill. Evenly built stone fences enclosed trim buildings and also two small fields, one with some sheep and lambs, three cows and two calves, and two small horses—one a mare with foal. In the other field, green corn shone in the sunlight. Beyond this, sloping up the hill, was a small fenced-in pasture and a field of young turnips in rows.

Immediately in front of the boys a geo, or gully cut into the cliffs, and at the far side there was a mound on the headland, high land that jutted out into the sea.

"Is that mound a burial place or an earth house, Mansie?"

"That's the Meerigeo howe—a burial mound. The Norsemen buried their dead in howes, or hollows."

"Is there one at the farm of Howe?"

"Aye, that's why it has its name."

On the near side of the geo, the boys found another kelp pit, neatly lined with stones and with rows of raised stones around the rim for ventilation, seemingly. Tangle-weed was piled on stone squares nearby, and heaps of a dry seaweed called ware lay all around, ready for burning. Below, on the rocks, lay an old dinghy, tarred all over like the boat that had taken them from the *Sigurd*, but smaller. Pulled up on the sand lay a fine yawl tied by a rope to an anchor high up on the beach. Nearby stood a line of lobster creels, and a man was in the act of putting down two more. He straightened up and turned to go back to the yawl.

He was a tall, slim, bearded man wearing a sailor's cap. As he looked up, he saw the boys, and watched them as they descended a path down a grassy bank and ap-

27

proached him. His face was pleasant, giving the lads confidence.

"Well, boys, and where may ye be going?" His voice was deep and kindly, his dark blue eyes steady.

Mansie looked at the man in his brown shirt and trousers, stammered, and stopped. Erchie timidly ventured, "We're looking for Walbreck, and a man called Oliver Ward."

"Ye're from the Sooth, I warrant," said the man, gazing steadily at them.

"Yes—that's it. I'm from Edinburgh. I'm Erchie Ward, and this is my cousin Mansie."

"Ward! That's grand. Ye'll be the boys o' me cousin that sailed and settled in Leith or Edinburgh. My! It's years since he came to see me. Ye're up on your holiday, I warrant."

"Yes, I am, Mr. Ward, and we've come to see you, for—"

"Bless me, boy, I'm no *Mister* Ward! That the truth. My name is Ollie. Selkie they call me. I'll take the last two creels up, for I'm drying and mending them, and we'll go right up to the hoose. A Ward is a Ward to me, and me to him, I hope."

Erchie looked at Mansie. Mansie looked at Erchie. They had found Selkie Ward! But this man, striding along with the creels, was surely not their great-great-grandfather? He looked younger than either of their fathers. And where was the village, and where was Mansie's home? At the cliff top they searched again. No village was to be seen.

Chapter 4

SELKIE AND FAMILY

AS OLLIE AND THE BOYS approached the barn, a group of six little boys gathered at the gable end. They varied a little in size from the biggest down to the smallest, a toddler, and all were tubby. They wore gray shirts and brown knee pants, and all stood looking unblinkingly at Erchie and Mansie with large, brown, liquid eyes underneath brown eye-brows and above rosy cheeks.

"Seawife and me have seven sons," said Selkie. "The youngest just a baby in the hoose."

"Hello, boys," greeted Erchie, "waiting for Daddy?"

The six little fellows all looked down at their bare feet, but did not answer.

"They're no whit ye could call forward," laughed Selkie. "Look up, Mathew; thoo're the eldest and speak to thee big cousins come to see us from Edinburgh. Look up, Mark, Luke, John, and Jeems, and peerie Andrew. I called them after the apostles," added Selkie in a low voice. "The wife comes o' heathen folk, ye ken."

An awkward silence was broken by John going to Erchie, taking his hand, and leaning against him. Little

Andrew toddled to Mansie, and reached up to him. Both lads noted how warm the children were to the touch.

"There can only be one year between them," said Erchie.

"That's all. I got me wife seven years ago past August, when the corn was ripening, and we had a son every May till last year. But comes the first o' May this year we had peerie Peter, and he's nearly two months old. Boys, are ye no speakin' to your cousins?"

John, who had been staring at Erchie's feet, looked and said, "Grand buits!" His brothers chuckled loudly.

"My boots," exclaimed Erchie, looking down at his dusty brogues. "They're not very grand, John."

"Thoo has thee own buits, Johnno," said Selkie.

"Me too!" came from one after the other, and even little Andrew lisped last of all, "Me got grand buits."

"Aye," said Selkie, "the wife got them buits, but they would sooner go in their bare feet, even in winter. They think the buits are over warm."

"So do I," said Mansie, "and I would not have these on today if it was not for . . . not for . . ." To his relief further explanation was unnecessary, for everyone had turned towards the cottage and was listening to a low-pitched voice singing what seemed to the boys to be the sweetest song.

> Lap a leedie, peerie darling,
> Pan a lappee, sealy joy;
> Selpa felkie, sea's a swaa-ing,
> Lap a leedie, peerie boy.

"That's Seawife singing to the little boy Peter," explained Selkie, walking over the flagstones to the cottage,

30

followed by all the boys. "Come oot, Wife," he called, "and see who's come to visit us."

A short, plump form glided out through the low door and approached. Her brown hair, almost chestnut and glinting in the sun, hung down over her greenish blouse to below her waist and over her gray homespun skirt. Erchie and Mansie saw an olive-skinned face and large, round, liquid-brown eyes which looked first at their necks, then at their hands, and then smilingly so straight at them that they dropped their glances to her broad and bare short feet.

"Erchie and Mansie Ward's come to see us, Wife. They're children o' me cousin in the Sooth."

"Welcome, Erchie and Mansie, welcome, and glad I am to see you." Her voice was low and pleasant. "Come into our peerie hoose," she invited, fingering two large and curiously carved pieces of amber suspended from a green cord around her neck.

In a wonder of admiration, they followed her through the door, and behind them came Selkie and his six boys. The kitchen was floored with flagstones. A grate, with an oven at one side, stood raised below a wide chimney, and over it a cast iron kettle hung from a large hook attached to a chain that came down the chimney. Above, and at each side, hung cast-iron saucepans and a frying pan. There were two straw-backed armchairs, one with a hood, and straw-bottomed stools arranged around a large table. At one end was a deep chest for holding meal, on which were several small neatly tied bundles of coarse grass. Over this was a shelf full of old-fashioned plates and mugs. There was a spinning wheel in one corner, and in another the cradle with the baby. The one window, a four-paned sash, looked down to the sea.

31

Selkie pulled two chairs forward, and asked the boys to seat themselves. Then the little boys sat down, all but Andrew, for Selkie sat in an armchair and took the boy on his knee. Seawife busied herself with putting plates of oatcakes and mugs of milk on the table.

Mansie did not fear questions, knowing that they would not be asked any, but Erchie, afraid that he might have to tell how they got there and knowing it would sound incredible, hastened to ask about the old woman in the next cottage.

"Oh, Mrs. Dearness, poor body," answered Selkie. "She and Tam are very frail, and suffer wi' the rheumities. But they're grand neighbors, no like them that envy us for the fish we catch and the beasts we raise."

Mansie was looking intently at each of the boys, wondering which could be his great-grandfather. Not being able to decide, he went over to the cradle, and looked down at the sleeping pink face.

Peerie Peter, he said to himself. Peter me brother, Peter me uncle, Peter me grandfather. Aye, a Peter. Me great-grandfather is a bonny baby."

"Mathew, Mark, and Luke, ye'll sleep in the barn this night, and your cousins in the hoose," said Selkie.

"No, no," cried Erchie and Mansie together. "I want to sleep in the barn," declared Erchie. "Me, too," added Mansie.

"But boys, that would look very wrong, and the neighbors will get hold o' it."

"Neighbors!" exclaimed Erchie. "It's no affair of theirs."

"Whit says thoo, Seawife?" asked Selkie.

Mansie noted a faint flush on the olive skin. After a moment's hesitation she said in a low voice, "If the two boys want to sleep in the barn, Selkie, let them."

"I'll make ready a place," said Selkie. "The nights are warm, and we have plenty o' blankets, thanks to the wife. Noo, Seawife, tak' all the boys doon to the geo for a swim. It's a grand day. I'll draw water for the beasts, and I'll look in at the peerie boy to see he's fine."

The little boys jumped up in excitement. "They're grand swimmers, even Andrew," said Selkie with pride.

"You can swim like a fish, Luke?" asked Erchie.

"No that way," piped Luke. "A fish wags his tail."

"And an eel wags all over," added Mark as he followed Mathew through the door. Seawife took little Andrew on her back. Mansie picked up John and Erchie carried Jeems on his back. They raced after the older three boys, the fat, dumpy, warm little riders making sounds between a chuckle and a laugh. Down the path to the geo they all ran. The older boys reached the rocks first, threw off their clothes and flopped into the sea. With their arms held close by their sides, kicking up and down with their legs, they shot out into the middle of the geo and then, using their hands like flippers or rudders, turned and darted inward. Erchie and Mansie followed. John and Jeems, slower in getting their few clothes off, jumped in too. Seawife, coming with little Andrew, undressed him and dropped him into the sea, in which he swam easily but slowly.

Erchie and Mansie were swimming strongly. Mathew and Mark waited for them, then darted at them, touched them on the shoulder and said, "Picko!"

"After them, Erch," spluttered Mansie. "It's tag, but say 'picko.'"

The two boys found it all they could do to catch the others, and sometimes suspected the little fellows tried to be caught. In the water they had difficulty in telling which was Mathew and which Mark, but they played on happily

33

until they all grew tired and then they stood in the shallow water drying themselves in the sun.

Mansie and Erchie looked towards Seawife. She smiled at them. Beyond her, near the rock-edge, two heads appeared in the water.

"Erch," whispered Mansie, "the kelpies."

"Yes," breathed Erchie, "and staring at us."

The other boys looked from their cousins, out to sea, and back again. "Whit see you?" asked Mathew.

"Two heads. There! Like horses," murmured Erchie. The heads disappeared. "Didn't you see them?"

"Nay, there's nothing there," said Mathew.

When they had climbed back on to the rocks and were dressing, Mathew said, "Mother, Erchie said he saw two heads like horses in the water. Did thoo see them?"

Seawife looked curiously at the two boys. After a moment she said, "Nay, Mathew, I was watching you boys."

After dressing, they all sat down on a rock, the younger boys pressed close to Erchie and Mansie, Seawife sitting behind. Erchie turned to her, and caught a glint of sunlight shining through the chestnut hair. "I liked your song to the baby," he said. "Won't you sing it to us?"

She flushed with pleasure, put her two hands over the large amber beads, and was silent for a minute. Then she began to sing in a low voice.

> *Bare rock sloping to the sea;*
> *Breezes gently raise the hair.*
> *Wavelets clipped in the thread-white fringe*
> *Dip to show the tangle ware.*
>
> *Pup and seal cow play beyond;*
> *Bull seal, watchful, floats on guard.*

Fears touch not my halfling sons;
I keep house for Selkie Ward.

When the last note had died away, Erchie said, "Thank you." She smiled at him and rose. "Come children, home," and she picked up Andrew. "Don't bother with them, they can walk," she said to Erchie and Mansie.

"Oh, but they like a carry," said Mansie, picking up John as Erchie picked up Jeems, and they all went slowly back to Walbreck in the late afternoon sun.

Chapter 5

IN THE MOONLIGHT

THAT SAME NIGHT, after Selkie Ward's children had gone
reluctantly to bed, the boys retired to the barn. Tired after
their strange day, they lay down on the blankets over the
hay with their clothes on. Long they rested, side by side,
but could not sleep.

The door opening—on which there was no door—faced
the sea. Through it bright moonlight streamed. From the
shadows they stared at the beams, each trying to understand how they came to be in their great-great-grandfather's barn. What had happened to their home since
they had left the *Sigurd?*

"Full moon! Full tide! Johnsmas," murmured Erchie.

"Aye, and the kelpies besides," said Mansie.

Suddenly they heard a faint creak. And then another!
As if someone had opened the cottage door and shut it
again. No other sound came. They sat up, looked towards
the dwelling house, and listened intently. A dim figure
with long hair glided past the opening of the barn. The
long hair and the gliding motion could only belong to one
person: Seawife!

They waited. She did not glide back. Minute after minute went by. Mansie gave Erchie a nudge. The two boys slipped out into the light of the moon which silvered the sea from the eastern horizon to the cliff.

A light wind blew inland from the sea. Her hair rippling away from her face, Seawife stood still at the edge of the cliff, and then slowly disappeared as she went down the path to the sea.

Mansie nodded towards the crags and, step by step, the boys moved towards the edge of the cliff and peered downwards. For a time they could see only the outline of rocks against the spasmodic sparkle of the sea. Then a dark form glided into the full light of the moon as it reached its zenith and sat on a rock lapped by the full tide. For a time Seawife sat still, as if she were staring at the sea. Then she began to sway from side to side, and as she did so her curved arms were raised shoulder high and described a slow rolling motion. The boys watched, fascinated.

Suddenly Mansie whispered urgently, "Look in the sea, Erch."

"A seal!"

"Aye!"

The dark, round head moved gradually nearer the rocks, then stopped. Seawife's motions were now very slow, then ceased altogether, the sea wind rippling her hair, the sea glinting around the seal's head. For a moment nothing moved, then the head and shoulders of the seal reared out of the water. Mansie drew his breath in sharply. Erchie gasped. But Seawife did not move.

The seal sank until only the tip of its nose showed, then raised itself breast-high above the surface of the sea once more and in a haunting, mournful voice sang:

Co afla sealong
Co afla sealong
Eee eulie ee, ee eulie eee.

Seawife remained motionless and then, raising one hand to draw her long hair away from her face, she replied:

Ne sealong, ne sealong.
Abanie, abanie,
Selkie, me Selkie.

Raising itself even higher out of the water this time, the seal sang sadly back:

Eul ee dong, eul ee dong,
All adie, all adie.
Ee eulie eee, ee eulie eee.

It was a long time before Seawife answered in her low, sweet voice, turning away from the sea as she sang:

Ne refeu, ne refeu,
Abanie, abanie,
Selkie, me Selkie.

There was a long silence. Suddenly the seal streaked towards the shore and clumsily floundered over the rocks towards the motionless Seawife.

Fear struck into the hearts of the boys. The seal now heaved itself forward until it was close to Seawife's feet. Erchie could stand it no longer. He sprang forward shouting, "Go back! Off!" Mansie leaped after him, and the two ran as fast as they could down the path shouting "Ahrr, ahrr, ahrrr," for no words would come.

They reached the rocks to see the seal, in a series of frantic undulations, racing towards the sea into which it fell from the rocks with a smack, and then disappeared.

Seawife had fallen to her knees, her head dropped forward and her long hair hiding her face. The boys came, one to each side of her as she clutched the amber beads at her neck.

"Mrs. Ward! Mrs. Ward!" breathed Erchie.

Feebly she put out an arm to Erchie, and the other to Mansie. Gently they tried to raise her, but she sank back on the rock with a sigh. After a moment she stirred to rise, and the boys, their arms under hers, strained hard and managed to get her to her feet. Then, with her arms around their necks, the boys moved slowly and carefully over the seaweed-covered rocks and over the loose stones to the foot of the cliff, Seawife almost a dead weight between them.

They rested a short time, and then negotiated the narrow path sideways, all three close together. Bit by bit they angled up, fearful of one falling over and dragging down the others. Often they stopped on the long wind up the path, but at last reached the top. Seawife's legs gave way, and the boys gently lowered her to the turf. They sat down, one each side, supporting her.

Time went past. The moon, now past its zenith, shone on an empty sea whose surface was still sprinkled by a light inshore breeze. Seawife gave a long sigh and once more sought to rise. The boys helped her up. For a moment all three faced the moon. Then Seawife spoke, softly and sadly.

"The seventh time and me seventh summer wi' Selkie! And it's half ·gone. It is well now."

She fondled the two pieces of amber at her neck. "Selkie took them from the Meerigeo burial mound for me. They stop the pull o' the sea." She turned her back on the sea and on the moon, and the boys did the same. They each took an arm and walked with her to the door of the cottage. She removed her arms gently from theirs, bent down and kissed first Mansie and then Erchie, and glided in.

The boys saw the door shut behind her. They went back to the barn.

"The pull of the sea!"

"Aye, Erch, it's in our bone and blood."

They lay down on the blankets over the hay and were soon fast asleep.

Chapter 6

IN THE PIT REEK

BREAKFAST THE NEXT DAY was a quiet meal, Seawife being
very silent. Erchie and Mansie could think of little to say
and were relieved when Selkie said, "Weel, boys, I'm
goin' up the hill to see Jeems Lyall o' Trebs and Bob Odie
o' Skeldro to get the kelp rakes. Does either one o' you
want to come wi' me?"

"Aye, I'll come," said Mansie readily.

"And so will I," exclaimed Erchie, aware of Seawife's
embarrassment.

"I want to come too, Dad," cried Mathew, Mark, and
Luke together.

"Nay, children," said Seawife softly. "We're burnin'
a pit, and I want you to help me."

"A kelp pit?" asked Erchie.

"Aye, tangleweed and ware," Mathew told him.

"Will you be finished before we get back?"

"Nay, Erchie," said Seawife, smiling. "It'll burn the
day long."

Erchie, glad that he would not miss the burning, set
off to the hill with Selkie and Mansie. They passed

41

through the field where the little brown sheep were grazing, the lambs nibbling close to the ewes.

"We have a fine flock o' lambs this year. The wife's a grand hand wi' the beasts, and I've lost neither lamb nor calf since she came to me. Our cows are in the next field," he said, pointing with pride to some small, sleek red and white cattle.

They approached an untidy set of buildings. "This is called the Trebs," Selkie informed them. "Jeems Lyall is too fond o' the bottle, and his wife, a cousin o' mine on the mother side, is a lazy woman. They lost half o' their lambs this spring for want o' lookin' after. And, in the next hoose, called Skeldro, Rob Odie's none better. He's married to a Lyall, and Jeems and him drink, besides brewing it. But Bob's a good hand at the blacksmith work, and makes the kelp rakes for the laird. We all have the use o' them."

Two dirty and ragged little girls stared at the three approaching.

"Well, children, are your folks at home?" asked Selkie cheerily.

"Mother!" shrilled the larger girl. "The witch-wife's man!"

A small, dark-eyed slovenly woman came to the unpainted low door, rubbing her hands on a sack apron.

"Ollie Ward! You're by yourself, I hope—oh, and whose lads are those?"

"They're boys o' a cousin o' mine in the Sooth."

"Well, you're wise to take them with you when you leave the house. You'll find Jeems in the barn, Ollie. Now, boys," she turned to Mansie and Erchie, "I'd ask you in, you being my kin, but it's a sore time with us, and nothing's been right these seven years gone by.

42

But Ollie's prospered. Fat sheep and cows, and plenty o' fish."

Mansie, shifting from one foot to another, was edging to the barn. "His cattle and sheep do look fine," stammered Erchie.

"Aye, the devil takes care o' his own, as I tell Jeems. There's Bob Odie comin'." Up he comes whenever he has drink, and Jeems doesn't like it."

Erchie also began edging away, for another woman was approaching, a large, coarse-looking woman. Surely, Erchie hoped, she would claim no kin with him.

"My," went on Mrs. Lyall, "here's Nellie Odie. Well, Nellie, what brings you over?"

"Oh, the same thing," said Nellie Odie in a high, complaining voice. "It's to warn you. Bob's got two bottles, but I managed to get them away from him till night so that the day would no' be lost. He took the kelp rakes up to Jeems in case he would be wantin' them. Or maybe Selkie wants them?"

"Aye, he's here for them, and I shall see his wife's smoke risin' at the crags," said Mrs. Lyall.

"Aye, aye, the kelp goes well for him, like everything else. There was a day when more than kelp would be burnin' and with a worse smell," added Nellie, giving the boys a strange, sideways glance, "for witch-women used to be burned."

"You lost five lambs this spring, too, Nellie," said Mrs. Lyall, slightly changing the subject.

"Aye, I did. Selkie lost none. Oh, it's well known, it's well known."

Erchie and Mansie, seeing a chance, hurried off to the barn where Selkie was standing with a large, fair, red-faced man and a tall, dark, yellow-eyed fellow. Two boys,

43

ragged and dirty, lounged nearby. They stared offensively at the younger Erchie and Mansie, looking them over from head to foot.

"No, I must go to my work, but thanks all the same," Selkie was saying.

"Well, the two of us will come wi' the rakes at dayset, and give thee a hand at slappin' doon the pit."

"Many thanks to you both, but . . . Noo, noo, boys, no fighting!"

Erchie, harassed by the younger Odie boy, who had just been poking and pulling his jacket, had struck down the boy's hand, and pushed the heel of his right hand to the boy's jaw. The boy had jerked back astonished.

"As I was sayin'," continued Selkie. "I must go to my work. Come away, boys."

Erchie and Mansie turned away gladly, but as Erchie did so, Willie Odie, the older boy, ran at him and slapped him on the back of the head. Erchie wheeled around to repay the slap, but Bob Odie called, "None o' that, Willie. Pick on boys o' thee age."

Selkie and the boys walked in silence until they were well out of hearing by these men and boys, and then Mansie asked, "Do they drink all the time?"

"There's whiles when they work and whiles when they have none, but they're at it often enough. I was as bad as them once, and in the past seven years the craving's come back, and I've had a sore time o' it. Seawife will no like to see the two o' them come with the kelp rakes, but it's a neighborly act, and we don't get many neighbors coming to see us."

"All the neighbors will no be like them," said Mansie.

"No, but most o' them like a drink, which they don't get with me. Some o' the women don't like Seawife, and clash among themselves. Their men make excuses when I

44

do well at the fishing and with the farm and they don't. Or the wives make excuses for them. I don't know which."

The acrid reek from the burning kelp pit was blowing in from the cliff, and as they approached, they saw Mathew and Seawife hold up a wheelbarrow with a sack on it over the weather side of the fire, to create a low draught. She had a black shawl over her hair, and wore an apron of sacking to protect her clothes. Her face was red from the heat, as was Mathew's. Mark and Luke were dashing through the smoke, back and forth, and coughing.

"Did thoo no get the rakes?" she asked Selkie.

"No, Bob said that he and Jeems would come with them at dayset, and give us a hand."

"Oh," said Seawife shortly. Then she added, "We've managed by ourselves many a day. More fair they put their hand to their own work."

"True, Wife, true, but it's a neighborly thought."

"I hope it is," murmured Seawife, looking into the smoke, her round eyes moist. "Well," she continued, "I'll go and look at the children and will be back with a bite to eat. It's near the height o' the sun."

She went to the cottage, and Selkie seized a fork and began energetically to move piles of seaweed near the pit so that they would be handy for burning. His three boys sat on the grass, silent and watching. Erchie and Mansie also watched as Selkie plugged the holes of glowing ashes as soon as they appeared. Then, with thick smoke pouring from the pit, he and Mathew held up the wheelbarrow on the lee side to draw the fire to the plugged holes.

"Did you carry all this seaweed up the path from the shore?" asked Erchie.

"Me, and the wife. Many a trek up we had wi' the tangleweeds in winter and wi' wheelbarrows o' ware in the spring."

"Can Erchie and I take in those for you?" asked Mansie, pointing to far piles of seaweed.

"Aye, you can do that. Take the other wheelbarrow and the fork."

For a time the boys carried in loads of seaweed and dumped them near the pit, and when all was in, they sat with Selkie's boys watching him feed the fire with armfuls of tangleweed and forkfuls of ware. All around them the grass was studded with violets and crowfoot. Overhead and inland larks sang, creating a web of music in the air.

Then all the boys faced the sea. A tern, with its forked, swallowlike tail, hovered momentarily in the air then dropped like a plummet, flicked the surface of the sea and, some small fish or morsel of food in its beak, flew upward with the characteristically rapid beat of its finely tapered wings. On the sea two eider ducks and their family cruised along, uttering their soft, almost human cries.

Mathew, Mark, and Luke became restless and showed excitement and Mansie exclaimed, "Here come the selkies!"

Splashing and bobbing, a number of seals of all sizes approached the rocks.

"We'll go and swim," said Luke.

"Will your mother let you?" asked Mansie, who wanted to go.

"Oh, I think she would," said Erchie. "We all played in the sea yesterday. Won't she, Mathew?"

Mathew turned his head to the cottage, gazed intently in that direction, seemed to listen, and then sniffed the air. "Aye, Mother will let us," he declared solemnly.

All five boys immediately ran down to the water's edge, undressed and plunged in. After splashing around they noticed the little seals drawing nearer and nearer, raising their heads out of the water and then diving as soon as they knew they were watched. The boys began playing "picko" and the seal pups drew nearer. One after the other the seal pups joined in, plunging, rising, rolling, gliding, and weaving to and fro as the boys tried to tag them. Selkie's sons did tag some, but Erchie and Mansie did not, and became so tired that they crawled out and dressed. Mathew, Mark, and Luke followed. Two seal pups, small and white in their first year coats, gazed at them with large, brown liquid eyes as though in disappointment, and then plunged down and vanished.

"Come up, now, boys," called Selkie from the cliff top. The boys looked up. Selkie, Seawife with peerie Peter, John, Jeems, and Andrew were all looking down at them and laughing.

When Mathew, Mark, Luke, Erchie, and Mansie reached the cliff top, Seawife had eggs cooking in the ashes, and a straw basket full of scones and oatcakes, all buttered, and milk—in bottles from Selkie's drinking days. They all sat on a bank eating, too contented to speak, Selkie occasionally attending the pit in which the last of the seaweed had nearly been consumed. So they sat till late afternoon, when Selkie began to sing:

> Noo the sparkle's geen oot o' the sea,
> In the afternoon when the breeze dies doon.
>
> Green and purple splash across the bay,
> And the smell's gone weak in the tangle reek.
>
> A' the wild birds flying to their homes,
> To the fulmar's rest, to the puffins nest
> Me and Seawife sit wi' our seven boys
> Near the Viking's howe, in the kelp pit's glow.

The happiness of the day was dampened for a time in the evening when Jeems Lyall and Bob Odie came with the kelp rakes and a spade. The two men looked at the pit.

"It's ready for raking, Ollie."

"Aye, Jeems."

"Well, start in," said Bob Odie.

The three men started pushing and pulling their rakes through the glowing ashes, moving slowly in a circle, making sure that all unburned seaweed was mixed in with the hot mass. Seawife followed with the spade, throwing spilled ash back into the pit. All four worked around and around for twenty minutes, sweat trickling from their bodies. Then Selkie took the spade from Seawife and clapped all the ashes down firmly. They could now be left until the ships from the South came to collect the kelp and take it away to some manufacturer who would use it as an ingredient for soap or glass.

Bob Odie and Jeems Lyall, who had not spoken or looked towards Seawife, took the implements and prepared to go.

"A good pitful, Ollie. Half a ton or more," said Bob.

"A little less, I think. Thanks, boys, for your help."

"Oh, thoo'll do as much for us another day," said Jeems.

After hidden glances at Seawife, who was staring at the pit, the two men moved off.

"They did not try to get thee wi' them," said Seawife in a low voice.

"No wi' thee here," laughed Selkie. "They have the drink again, and will be wantin' to get at it."

In the near-twilight the family walked back to the cottage, Erchie carrying peerie Peter in his cradle, and Mansie hand in hand with Jeems and Andrew.

Chapter 7

MOTHER'S BROTHER

"KEEP OOT O' THE SEA, BOYS," admonished Selkie as his two visitors and three eldest sons set off the next day to explore the shore beneath the cliffs. "There's been two killer whales around. I've not seen one for twenty years."

"Aye," answered Mansie, "we'll keep to the ebb."

"And the sky's no so good," continued Selkie. "Make for home if the weather comes down on ye."

The five boys took the path down from Meerigeo Howe to the shore and walked over the rocks to the headland. With the sea at half-ebb, a miniature world of valleys and rock mountains was uncovered, and as the water gurgled down little falls and tinkled towards the sea, the boys in their bare feet waded round the headland to Quoyness.

Little Luke, who was with Erchie and a little behind the others, cupped his hands to his mouth and boomed out "Ee-hoo-oo-ee-hoo-ee."

Mathew turned to his young brother, "Nay, Luke, you must no call the selkies."

"Can you talk with the seals, Luke?" asked Erchie.

"Not very well. But mother's brother can."

"Hush, Luke," whispered Mathew.

Mother's brother! Erchie looked keenly at Luke's little round face as the eyes gazed seaward, and then at Mansie. Mother's brother! "Does he live with the seals, Luke?" he asked.

"Nay, nay," said Luke, "he lives under the ground all by himself when the selkies aren't with him."

"Stow, Luke!" ordered Mathew suddenly, and grasping Luke's hand, he pulled him aside.

The sand, soft from the ebbing of the waters, squelched between the toes of the five boys as they walked slowly on. They examined empty shells—limpet, cockle, crab, scallop, silver willie, and rose tellen, and surprised tiny eels, periwinkles, and shore hoppers that slept during the ebb.

"Here's a sea urchin," cried Erchie, holding up a round, prickly object.

"And stiff whiskers on his head like mother's brother," laughed Mark.

"Mark!" Mathew pulled him aside as he had done Luke. "You mustn't speak of him. Folk will find out where he lives and pester the life out of him and kill the selkies."

Erchie and Mansie exchanged glances. The description of the stiff-whiskered head reminded them of Henry Goar who was not Henry Goar, but they said no more.

Finally they reached Hacksness Point, around which the water was deep enough for killer whales to come in and chase the seals right up to the rocks.

"Mansie!" whispered Erchie, pointing to the sea. "The kelpies!"

"Aye! I saw them," muttered Mansie.

"What are you talking about?" asked Mark.

"Kelpies," said Erchie. "Look!"

50

Mathew looked, and then turned to Erchie. "I see nothing."

Within a few moments the wind began to rise and rain began falling. Mathew was pressing forward impatiently, not liking to remind Mansie and Erchie that they should hurry home if it began to storm.

"There's a small boat coming through the tide, Erch."

"Aye," said Mansie, "and I hope the boatman makes it," he added as the white-crested waves seemed to claw at the craft and rob the oarsman of control.

"It'll never bother him," declared Mathew calmly.

"Do you know the boatman?" asked Erchie.

"Aye." Mathew and his two brothers turned their backs to the sea and started to walk inland. "Father said to come home when it rained."

A stiff east wind was now blowing, casting spray over the rocks, and the rain pelted down. The boys started to run homeward—all but Erchie. "Here comes the boatman driving like fury into the wind," he cried as one lash of saltwater spray hit him about the face.

The four other boys stopped, turned, and stared.

A thick-set man stood in the small boat, guiding it forward calmly through the foaming breakers with skillful twists and flicks of a single oar over the stern. Nearer he came and nearer, sometimes surfing forward at high speed, until he was almost onto the rocks and it seemed as though his boat would smash onto them.

Mathew, Mark, and Luke ran back and scrambled down towards him.

"Take care, Mathew!" shouted Erchie, as he and Mansie followed. "Luke will fall if you don't watch." For he was fearful that the little boy would tumble and dash his head against a sharp rock. They reached the shore and, clustered together with the three other boys in the driving rain, stared at the man in the pitching boat.

"Whale's gone north!" he shouted above the roar of the sea. "Selkies are safe."

"Aye!" answered Mathew.

The little boat plunged and twisted, but the man stood firm on his short legs. He looked out of his black eyes first at Erchie and then at Mansie. It was a friendly look that seemed to hold recognition. Then he turned and, with a powerful thrust on the single oar, wheeled his craft seaward.

Suddenly Mansie recognized him. "Erchie! Erchie! It is Henry Goar!"

Erchie started. "Henry!" he shouted.

Briefly the little boatman turned his head. "Nay, boys, nay. But I'll see ye again anyway."

The rain suddenly fell down like a thick curtain across the sea and hid the boat.

"He's mother's brother," repeated Mathew.

"Mother makes his clothes for him," said Mark.

"Your mother does?" asked Erchie.

"Aye, she spins and knits."

No one spoke for a while, then Mathew's curiosity got the better of him. "You knew him before?"

"Yes, Mathew, long ago," answered Mansie. "Or it seemed long ago," he added.

"The day afore yesterday?" asked Luke after a pause.

Mansie looked around. They were enclosed in a tent of rain beyond which drummed an endless sea. "I don't know, Luke. It might be the day after tomorrow."

Luke laughed. "The day after tomorrow! You knew him tomorrow!" He laughed again, and Mathew and Mark looked at him and also began laughing.

As soon as the five boys drew near the cottage, Luke waddled ahead over the flagstones to the front door calling, "Mother! Mother! The selkies are safe now, for the whale's gone north. So thee brother says."

Seawife appeared at the door and looked anxiously at the rain-drenched boys.

"Aye," Mathew assured her, "your brother came in to the rocks and spoke to us."

Seawife smiled at Erchie and Mansie. "You boys saw my brother?"

"Yea," piped Luke, "and Mansie says he saw him the day after tomorrow!" Luke flung himself into his mother's arms and both laughed together, but then Seawife murmured to him, "But Mansie did no say it for fun, Luke."

"The boys don't call him uncle," remarked Erchie.

"Nay, Erchie, for he's no me real brother. I just say that to the children."

"Oh, I see," answered Erchie, puzzled.

That night in the barn the boys lay silent for a time, unable to sleep, each preoccupied with his own thoughts. Then Erchie said, "I had thought that we might be related to Henry Goar."

"If it is Henry Goar," said Mansie. "But I think we're related close to Seawife."

"Yes, and she's a mystery to me."

"Take things as they come, Erch."

Chapter 8

THE STORM

EARLY THE NEXT MORNING Mansie and Erchie were awakened by a gale that gusted through the open doorway and threatened to lift the heavy stone slates off the rafters. Smoke swirling from the cottage chimney told them that someone was astir, so they got up and dressed. The moment they were outside, they were smitten by an easterly wind and were instantly propelled towards the cottage.

Seawife was giving peerie Peter his bottle. "Tak' the big chairs, boys, for you must be bone chilled," she said indicating the straw-backed armchairs near the fire. They thanked her, and sat watching the baby in his cradle sucking at his bottle, his large brown eyes on the ceiling, completely undisturbed by the sound of the wind wailing around the cottage. Mathew, Mark, Luke, John, James, and Andrew now gathered around, and all gazed solemnly into the fire. All of them seemed to be anxious about something, and when they sat around the table for their porridge, they were silent. Selkie had not appeared. Neither Mansie nor Erchie could bring himself to ask why.

When the meal was almost over, a heavy tread sounded above the wail of the wind, and Selkie clumped in, his clothes glistening with salt spray.

"All five o' them's drowned," he announced in low tones to his wife.

For a moment no one spoke, then Selkie continued. "Erchie and Mansie, ye were sleeping and do not know."

For a moment the wind abated, and there was complete silence.

"A ship went past in the night firing rockets," continued Selkie, "and tore down to Hacksness. I knew she had run into something, for there were no more rockets. I went out about three in the morning when day was breaking and down to Hacksness as fast as I could. She had swirled around the point, after hitting, and gone to pieces. A schooner from Narrawa. Jock Maitland and me dragged five bodies out. There weren't any more."

After a little while Seawife asked, "Didn't Jeems Lyall and Bob Odie help?"

"They were afraid o' the bodies. They said it was bad luck to touch them. Like the old folk, they think if a sailor is dead on land, that's him dead. But if he's drowned, he lives on."

"No help wi' the bodies!" exclaimed Seawife. "There might still have been life in them."

"They'll keep warm enough for a while with the driftwood they collected," said Selkie bitterly.

Suddenly Mathew, who had been standing near the window shouted excitedly, "A ship's come stirin' round the point!"

"She's not being steered!" cried Mansie, as they all crowded together, staring towards the sea.

"What can have taken them!" exclaimed Selkie as the sloop, its mainsail billowing out on the port side as it ran before the wind, veered, for a moment stood in irons, and then jibed and drove on in towards the shore.

"She'll strike the southeast point unless she jibes again," said Selkie, and just as the sloop seemed certain to ride straight on to the foaming rocks, she jibed again and was carried past the point.

"We'll go to them," cried Seawife. "They must be too feared for anything."

"But Seawife, two of us can't handle it. We need three."

"I'll come," said Mansie. "I can handle sails."

"I'll come too," said Erchie.

"You know little about boats," Mansie reminded him.

"Stay with the children, Erchie," commanded Selkie, "and Seawife will come with me. She's a grand hand in a boat. Come now or we shall be too late."

"The sloop will be on the reef any minute!" cried Mansie, and the three hurried out, leaving Erchie with the children.

Selkie's yawl, the *Kittiwake* was tossing at her land anchor, but sheltered by the headland from the heavy seas. Selkie pulled her in, Mansie clambered aboard and set up the mast while Seawife bolted on the rudder. Then Selkie pushed off, boarded, seized an oar, and shouted to Mansie to take the helm. Seawife seized the other oar, and, both rowing strongly, the *Kittiwake* plunged into the unsheltered sea.

"She's missed the reef," shouted Mansie, "and is headed for the west tail o' the holm."

Selkie took both oars while Seawife tied the reef points in the sail and then hoisted it. Mansie, feeling the way on the boat, hauled the sheet tight and the *Kittiwake* leaped forward, lying close to the wind.

"I'll take her now, Mansie," said Selkie, coming to the tiller. "You're doing fine, but I've known this boat for a long time." Mansie moved to the mid-thwart, and Seawife sat on the forward one.

The sloop was veering about, caught first by one billow and then by another, and now drifting rapidly towards Hacksness, the fallen mainsail billowing from one side to the other with the wind.

"Change the sail," ordered Selkie, "for I can weather her now," and he ran the yawl into the wind. Down came the sail as Seawife loosened the rope connected to the mainsail, and she and Mansie quickly changed it and hoisted it again. The *Kittiwake*, now in heavier seas, rose high on the billows and then crashed down scattering the broken waters under the impact. Mansie was thrilled to see how the boat behaved and how Selkie managed to dodge the higher waves. Tearing through the water at a great rate, they were now rapidly nearing the sloop.

"One o' us must board her," shouted Selkie. "It'll be a critical job."

"I'll do it," shouted Mansie. "It will take a good jump. The bowsprit will be the place when she jibes again."

"Can you steer that sloop?" asked Selkie.

"Yes, but I can't handle that mainsail by myself."

"Well, signal if you need me. I'll weather her and come in. Change places with him, Seawife."

Mansie got up on the forward thwart and the *Kittiwake* plunged forward to the sloop as it jibed around. Selkie rounded the stern and sent his yawl alongside.

"Look spry, Mansie," called Selkie, and he cut across the sloop's bow. For a moment Mansie felt the bowsprit stays would foul the yawl's mast, but the boat glided forward, and Mansie sprang. He clutched the stay, got a grip with both hands, and swung himself up. Astride the bowsprit, he crawled back, and dropped on to the deck.

No sailor was in the bow. Mansie crawled carefully over the billowing canvas of the mainsail to the small space aft. There, under the yard, lay a short, thick-set man, his forehead clotted with blood. A sailor's hat, clutched in one hand, showed that he was the skipper.

With breath held tight, Mansie passed the body, seized the wheel, and, with a struggle, righted the vessel, steering for Meerigeo. He could not see the *Kittiwake,* but he remembered her tacking and knew she was following. Letting go of the wheel for an instant he signaled frantically, and again took the wheel to guide the sloop under her two jibs or three-cornered sails.

"Gid-gad!" sounded behind him, and he half-turned to see Selkie step over the stern, his gaze on the fallen sailor.

"Follow Seawife to the geo, Mansie, for we must drop the anchor just at the weather side o' the rocks, and trust she'll swing safe."

"Aye, I'll keep right in her wake," said Mansie.

"And as soon as I drop anchor, run her right into the geo."

"Aye."

Selkie crawled over the mainsail and stood at the bow, only his head visible to Mansie. But the boy heard the chain rattle out, waited until the sloop was beyond the breakers, and then ran her into the geo. He waited breathless as the anchor dragged and the sloop moved to the rocks on the lee side, but she spun around, steadied, and tossed at her anchor, safe in Meerigeo.

Chapter 9

THE SLOOP'S CREW

SELKIE AND MANSIE went to the fallen man, and Selkie bent down and put his hand inside the man's clothes. After a while he said, "His heart's beatin' no so bad. We'll bear him to his cabin. Beats me where his men are. Take his feet, Mansie." Selkie went to the side and shouted to Seawife to come aboard. Then he seized the man below the armpits, and he and Mansie staggered with the burden to the hatch. It was very small, the steps narrow, and they had to go slowly down to a door that stood ajar. A lantern burned dimly within the cramped space, showing a bunk and an open storage chest. Mansie kicked something hard with his bare toe, and winced. Then they rolled the man into the bunk, and looked around. The open chest showed a square for four bottles—rum or brandy likely—and it was empty. Mansie picked up the object he had stumbled over. It was an empty rum bottle. Selkie shook his head.

They looked to the man. He stirred and groaned. Seawife entered. Selkie told her briefly what they had found.

"The crew?" she asked.

"Who knows. Drunk, and knocked overboard by the sail, like enough." Selkie indicated the empty bottle and the empty spaces in the chest.

"The name on the bow is *Skua*," said Seawife. "I'll get some water and wash the blood away." She went on deck to the small water kegs.

Selkie and Mansie watched the man as he slowly opened his gray eyes and stared dazedly at them. Seawife returned, swabbed the wound, and said, "It's a shallow cut. He's been knocked stupid by the yard."

The man muttered.

"Eh? What's that?" asked Selkie.

"Is my ship wrecked?" he moaned, a little louder.

"No. You're safe in Meerigeo."

"Meerigeo?" The man sat up.

"Aye, on the east side o' Sanday. Where's thee men?"

"My men?" The man breathed heavily, and looked at the open chest.

"Were they washed overboard?"

"Drunken scum! Not them!" he hissed.

The three waited while he got his breath. "When the storm struck, they crowded in here yelling that we were lost, and left me at the wheel." He breathed heavily again and went on. "I ordered them on deck to reef." Again he paused. "They came up with the bottles, and one went to the upper deck. The other two just let go the halyard and ran there. Then something struck me, and that's the last I can remember."

He was speaking now in a loud, domineering voice, his words tumbling over each other. His round, weather-beaten face was getting back its ruddy color, helped with the anger he felt. "Give me a drink," he ordered.

"Get one from the water cask," Selkie said to Seawife.

60

"Not that blash! Rum, man, rum."

Selkie pointed to the chest with its empty compartment.

"Aye, I forgot. But there's plenty a . . ." He stopped, and considered. "We'll go forward to see what these whelps are like," he said grimly, and got to his feet, testing his legs. Then he signaled to the three to leave before him. They went on deck. Seawife went to the stern, pulled on the *Kittiwake's* painter, brought her alongside, and jumped aboard.

"You'd better go as well, Mansie," said Selkie in a low voice. Mansie clambered into the *Kittiwake* which drifted to the end of her painter, rocking and swaying. He and Seawife watched Selkie and the skipper crawl over the sail to the bow of the sloop.

"I was sure nobody was steering her," said Mansie.

"Oh, the drink!" exclaimed Seawife. "Men like that leavin' their work. It's awful."

Some yells sounded from the bow of the *Skua* above the roar of the surf, and the two waited anxiously. After a while, Selkie appeared at the stern, pulled in the yawl, clambered down, and took the oars. Then as he rowed into the sand, he said, "The three men were dead drunk. A fat big fellow, the mate, and two short lads about twenty. The skipper shook them and kicked them till they yelled. When they had come to, he ordered them on deck to stow the sails. I said I would help, and he says, 'Leave these whelps to me. They made this mess and they'll clear it up.' Seeing I wasn't wanted, I came away."

"Did the skipper seem to have his strength back?"

"Well, he can kick strong enough," said Selkie grimly. "Let's go home. They're a coarse lot, and the mate's afraid of the two young fellows, the skipper says."

The three went silently up the path and on to the cottage where Erchie and the children crowded at the door. "Are the men safe?" inquired Erchie anxiously.

"Safe enough and drunk enough," said Mansie.

They went in and took off their wet clothes. "Go to the ben and take off yours," said Seawife to Mansie, "and put a blanket about you, and we'll dry them at the fire. I'll warm some milk."

"I saw you get on the ship, Mansie," said Erchie.

"Did you, Erchie," said Selkie, "and was it no well done?"

Glowing with pleasure, Mansie went into the ben room, which is the name for the inner room of a cottage. It was a rather bare room with two box beds in it, two straw stools, and a straw settee. He took off his wet clothes, pulled a blanket out of one of the beds, wrapped it around him, and came back to be given a seat by the fire. He watched the steam rise off his wet clothes, and felt quite shivery for a short time. But he slowly warmed up, and felt pleasantly tired.

Little was said, the strange condition of the sloop being a disappointment to them after their efforts to save it. After a short time, a man came to the door.

"Come in, Willie Sinclair," invited Selkie. "Did you make the boxes for the bodies?"

"Aye," said Willie Sinclair, who looked very solemn. "But first, I saw thee and thee wife board the sloop and take her in safe. It was grand work. And is this the lad that jumped to the bowsprit?" he asked, indicating Mansie.

"Aye, Willie, and did he no do it well?"

"Faith he did," said Willie readily, and Mansie blushed at the praise. "I thought the crew would be here," he went on.

"The men are in no fit shape," said Selkie. "The three were dead drunk, and the skipper felled by the yard. We brought him to, but he did no want us around."

"Aye, man. One o' them again," murmured Willie. "We're taking the bodies you and Jock brought ashore in the morn. There's no a thing to tell their names, and their faces are a' smashed in beyond recognizing. We'll bury them in the unknown sailors' part of the yard. You'll come and help us give them a decent burial."

"Of course, Will. Need you ask?"

"I'll go and see if the others will come. One o' the clock, mind!"

"I'll be with you," said Selkie sadly as Willie went away. "That's Willie Sinclair o' Whupland," explained Selkie. "He's made the boxes for coffins with all the wood he had."

They were very quiet after this. Erchie had imagined drowned sailors as whole men, like a man drowned in a harbor basin whom he had seen. He shuddered to think of a face being battered on the rocks with all the force of the wild sea.

"The sloop's crew are a queer lot, Seawife," said Selkie, "but I'm glad I didn't have to drag them out o' the sea with their faces battered."

Chapter 10

THE *SKUA'S* DINGHY

THE WIND DIED DOWN during the night, and the next morning was bright and calm.

"I'll have a look at the sloop to see that all's well with them," said Selkie.

"Will they welcome your asking, do you think?" inquired Seawife.

"I doubt it, but they should be sober now. Do you want to come, boys?"

"Aye," came from all the boys. Erchie added, "Yes, for we can go along the beach and see what the storm has done."

"John, Jeems, and Andrew, ye'll come with peerie Peter and me to see Mrs. Dearness, for I'm taking some milk to her," said Seawife.

Selkie and the five boys came to the cliff top and saw the *Skua* riding quietly at anchor in Meerigeo. The mainsail had been furled, showing a dinghy on deck over the hatch and a windlass and derrick by the mast.

"She looks like the sloops that carry slate from Thurso," Selkie remarked.

"Slates like those on your house?" asked Erchie.

"Aye, but I doubt if she's carrying any slates. She's not loaded deep, and she would no have come 'round Elsness if she had a cargo o' slates aboard."

"There's a man on deck, Dad," said Mathew, gazing with his round eyes at the cabin hatch.

The man came on deck and walked around the vessel.

"We'll go down on the rocks," said Selkie. "Maybe they need some milk and eggs."

Selkie went slowly down the path followed by the boys, and slowly across the sand of the geo to the rocks beneath the headland, glancing from time to time to the *Skua*. Quite near the sloop they stopped and looked at the young sailor aboard. He stared at them from a dark visage beneath a cloth cap, and scowled.

"You all right now?" inquired Selkie.

The sailor made no answer, but continued to scowl.

"Ye had a sore time o' it yesterday, and I thought I would ask," continued Selkie.

The sailor spat into the sea. "No doubt but you want to keep an eye on us," came in a growl from him. "We need none of your help. Go back to your barn."

Selkie shook his head, knowing what would have happened to the sailor had it not been for his help. Then he turned to the boys. "Ye're going 'round the shore, boys. I have to go to the burial. Now, don't watch this ship or the men, and come back above the banks."

"Aye," promised Mansie. "They're not the kind I want to go near."

Selkie went back to the path. The five boys stepped away quickly and leaped over the rocks, and only after they were around the headland and out of sight of the sloop did they amble on the sunlit beach where the incoming tide gurgled through little channels in the rocks, filling up the rock pools. They stood around these pools and watched the weeds stretch themselves and glisten brown, blue, green, and red. Little crabs came to life and scurried to pieces of shell fish killed in the storm. And the hoppers and sholties came out and darted between the colored pebbles. As the tide crept over the rocks, even the periwinkles seemed to move, and the bladder weed began to wave gently over the barnacles and limpets.

"They all sleep when the sea's out and wake up and get their meat when it comes in," explained Mark to Erchie.

Eventually the five boys came to Quoyness sands and waded in the shallow, sparkling water. They forgot the surly sailor as they gazed at the sandy, sunbeamed bottom. Mark signaled to Erchie to come and look at something. Erchie, thinking silence was needed, waded slowly to him and looked over the boy's shoulder. Two bright spots shone in the sand. Mark stooped down and scooped up a cockle. Then he put it back.

"Were those its eyes we saw, Mark?"

"Nay, its mouth. It gets its breakfast from the sea."

As the boys drew near the far side of the sands, they saw many seals on the rocks, two scrambling into the flood to begin their hunting. The others lay lazily around, raising a head occasionally to see if the tide was coming nearer. The boys quietly approached, little Luke first.

"Ee-hoo-oo ee hoo-oo ee-ee," he blew gently through his cupped hands.

Some seals raised their heads, looked at the boys, and then lowered them again. Baby seals gazed innocently and unafraid.

"Don't go too near the mother with pups," Mathew warned. "Keep back if they growl."

The boys went closer and stared into the large, round liquid eyes of the seals. Suddenly, one of the seals fluted a warning note and they all began scrambling over the rocks into the sea, the mothers calling their pups.

"They must be feared o' you, Mansie and Erchie," said Mathew.

"Not me," said Mansie, "and not Erchie, either."

"A boat's coming!" cried Erchie. "Isn't it the dinghy of the *Skua?*"

All five boys saw the dinghy being rowed around the head of the geo. It was coming straight to them.

"Your father wanted us to keep away from them," whispered Erchie.

"We'll go above the banks, and no delay," said Mansie. "That boat's deep loaded."

They scrambled up the twelve-foot bank, and went to a nearby enclosure for sheep. There, behind the low, broken fence, they watched the dinghy until it was hidden by the bank. After a time, curiosity got the better of them, and they all crept to the edge of the bank. One man was holding the boat in while another sat on the center thwart. A third, a large fat man, was wandering on the shore. Suddenly he looked up and saw the boys.

"You spying, tattling brats," he spat at them. "If I get my hands on you— . . ." He ran for the bank.

The boys turned and fled, Erchie catching Luke's hand and hurrying him on. Past the sheep enclosure they dashed, and up the slope to the fence along the hill. Here they stopped, all gasping for breath. The big, fat man shook his fist at them, turned back to the beach, and disappeared.

"That must be the mate your father spoke of," said Erchie.

"Good thing he's big and fat," said Mansie lightly, and

then seeing that the three little ones were frightened, he continued, "We'll go home now and keep to the land side o' the fence while we can."

As they drew near to Walbreck, Mathew said, "We'll not tell about this. Father said to keep away from them, and we went back to see what they were doing."

"Well, Mathew, we'll not tell. Not just yet," promised Mansie.

Chapter 11

THE *SKUA* DEPARTS

MANSIE AND ERCHIE AWAKENED in the morning to hear voices outside the barn.

"Well, Ollie, thee and thee wife got the sloop safe into the geo in the gale."

"Aye, Jeems, we managed. Though it was a critical job in times."

"Poor folk like us will have to do without the driftwood," said another voice, "and that's not neighborly."

"We're no wanting dead neighbors in the geo, Bob, and four men are alive that would have been drowned."

Another voice, strange to the boys, broke in. "Ollie— as they name you—tell those boys of yours not to pry around us, watching every little thing we do, or it will be worse for their health."

Mansie and Erchie crept to the doorway to see Jeems Lyall, Bob Odie, and the man who had threatened them at the beach the day before.

"Me boys!" exclaimed Selkie. "They were down with me for two or three minutes at your sloop yesterday. I told them to keep away from you and your ship, and I know they would have done it."

"I'm not talking of our ship," blustered the mate of the *Skua*. "They watched us in the boat beyond the sands and must have followed us. See there," he shouted, pointing to the doorway, "they're at it again. Come here, you young whelps!" He strode towards Mansie and his cousin, but Selkie leaped in front of him, and grabbing the sailor by the scruff of the neck, held him at arm's length.

"Lay no hand on them," Selkie growled, shaking the man. "If it was not that I saved thee from the sea, I'd make thee a sack o' sore bones."

The mate shook himself free and backed away, cowering.

"Peace, Ollie, peace," said Jeems Lyall. "The mate, poor man, has been at death's door, as you know."

Selkie stood back, and for a short time the four men stood in awkward silence. Then Bob Odie spoke, his yellow eyes darting from Selkie to the mate. "We'll come to the sloop with you, mate, and let Ollie get over his bit o' madness. Jeems and me will be seeing thee, Ollie, and thoo," he added menacingly, "might be seein' that it's an ill wind that does not blow somebody good."

The three men turned, walked to the crag and went down the path to the geo. When they were out of sight, Selkie turned on the boys. "What's this about you watching them?"

Mansie looked at Erchie, who spoke. "At the far side of Quoyness we saw their boat coming and, as you had warned us to keep clear of them, we went up on the beach to the old sheep's pen. We waited, and thinking they would be away again, crawled to the beach and looked over. The mate saw us and came running after us, but we ran to the hill fence and came home along the hill."

"Oh, was that all?"

"Aye," said Mansie quickly, "only we promised the boys not to tell, and now we've done it. Don't tell them we did."

Selkie laughed. "I'll not go into it," he promised.

"But why is the sailor so mad at us looking?" asked Erchie.

"You may well ask," answered Selkie. "I have my suspicions o' them, but the least said the better just now."

After breakfast, Seawife said, "We're needin' grass for the basket I'm making, Ollie, and for new horse traces. Tak' Erchie and Mansie wi' thee and go to the fields. I'll tak' the children wi' me up to Mrs. Dearness again; she's always glad to see them."

"Aye, Wife. Are ye comin' wi' me, lads?"

"Yes," said Erchie. Selkie got his sickle to cut the coarse grass needed for the traces, and the three set out towards Beasand, keeping away from the crags until they were some distance from the sloop. The day was fair and the lads looked over rippled Backaskaill Bay to Beaness where roofs and chimneys of the houses of Kettletoft should have been, but where there was nothing to be seen except the arms of the windmill.

"Their dinghy's coming 'round the head again, high in the water this time," announced Mansie.

"There's only one man in it," said Selkie, "but the men in the sloop are setting up the jibs."

"Bob Odie and Jeems Lyall aren't there."

"True, Erchie. Now where can they be I wonder," murmured Selkie. "We'll go on, for they don't want to be watched, and no doubt have good reason for it."

The three went down to the sands and along almost to the place where the gauger had hailed them and taken their sacks of chaff away. Then they went over the shore to the low sand dunes where the long grass grew. Selkie set to work with his sickle, selecting the longer-stalked grasses and then tying them into small sheaves.

Curious about the *Skua*, the boys stood on the dune, watching the sea.

"The sloop's moving out," cried Mansie. "The dinghy's towing her clear."

"Aye, I would not wonder," said Selkie, wielding his sickle and not looking up.

"They're hoisting the mainsail now," cried Erchie, but Selkie did not pause to look.

"But, see down at Spurness Holms," said Mansie excitedly, "a big boat's coming from Kirkwall."

Selkie looked up at last. "It's either a sloop or a cutter with the bowsprit run out," he observed.

Meanwhile the *Skua*, her mainsail and jibs drawing, was standing out across the bay in the direction of Elsness. The sloop or cutter which had turned in along the land at Hacksness, now slightly altered course and, making for the *Skua*, started to close in on her.

"A naval cutter," said Selkie. "Now I wonder . . ."

The three watched eagerly as the cutter, which was towing a dinghy and sailing farther seaward than the sloop, rapidly overhauled her to windward. The sloop, now about half a mile out from the edge of the sea, would soon have to tack if she wanted to clear Elsness Holm. The cutter drew nearer and nearer, and then the excited boys heard a hail from her to the sloop. The *Skua* ran into wind and stood to, her sails shaking. The cutter ran around, and five Navy men got into the dinghy and rowed to the sloop. Four of them boarded and then separated on the *Skua's* deck.

Shortly Selkie and the boys saw the crew of the *Skua*

72

join the one Navy man in the dinghy which returned to the cutter. Meanwhile the *Skua,* manned by the Navy men, headed around towards Kirkwall.

"Have they been arrested, and is a naval crew on the *Skua?*" asked Erchie.

"Of course, boy," said Mansie, "they're smugglers aren't they?"

"Aye, I suspicioned it," said Selkie shortly.

The cutter lay in the wind for a while, and then headed unexpectedly to Kettletoft Bay.

"Now where're they going?" asked Erchie.

"That I don't know," said Selkie. "You'd think they'd take the crew to Kirkwall for trial. Maybe they're seeking Webster the gauger. He lives in a house by Elsness. He should have been here long ago to look at the sloop, but he's over fond o' the drink himself. He'll get a keel-hauling I expect."

Mansie and Erchie looked at each other. The man on the pony who had stopped them in the King's name was in trouble himself—at least so Selkie thought.

Chapter 12

IN THE KING'S NAME!

SELKIE AND THE BOYS were looking down at Meerigeo, feeling glad the troublesome sloop was gone, when Mathew called his father's attention to a group coming down the hill towards them. One rode a pony, and on each side trudged one other man. When they drew nearer, Mansie and Erchie recognized the tall, dark, red-faced man on the shaggy pony as the gauger who had stopped them near the mill. The other two were Selkie's neighbors, Bob Odie and Jeems Lyall.

"Now, I wonder what's in the wind," murmured Selkie.

As the men reached them, the gauger stopped his pony and dismounted, while the bulky Jeems and the yellow-eyed Bob looked furtively from Selkie and the boys to the geo.

"Good-day to you, Selkie," said the gauger.

"And good-deen to ye, Mr. Webster."

"Ah, the two lads from the South," went on the gauger, recognizing Mansie and Erchie. "I hope you've not wanted sleep, Selkie, since I took the chaff for your bed from these boys." And he glanced sardonically at Erchie and Mansie.

"Chaff? What chaff?"

"Didn't they tell you that I took the chaff from them? Old Moodie saw me coming, and loaded two sacks of chaff on to these lads. I took his bait, and went after them, and when I got back to the mill, whatever malt Moodie had was well out of sight."

Selkie laughed loudly. "No, they told me nothing, knowing no doubt that they had been tricked, and not wanting to be laughed at."

Selkie stopped laughing, and as the gauger did not speak, he went on, "But what brings ye so early in the day, Mr. Webster? Ye'll find no malt at Walbreck."

"No, Selkie, I'm not here to search your house. The *Skua*, that sloop you brought in here, had illicit cargo, you know."

"I helped them to their anchorage, but I neither knew nor asked their business, though I had me suspicions."

"Well, the fat mate turned King's evidence and saved his own hide. There are three kilderkins of rum and one firkin of brandy buried on the beach near Quoyness. The rest of the cargo is seized and held by the naval cutter."

"Mighty! And did the mate tell you how to get hold of the drink they buried?"

"Oh, yes, he blurted everything in his fright. They were left to the care of these two rogues here, who say they were just going to come and tell me. Perhaps the court will believe them more than I do."

"We've done nothing you can lay to us, Mr. Webster," protested Jeems Lyall. "We have not used the drink, and will lead you to it, for we know where it is, as we would have done if you had waited."

"No doubt you could not come to me yesterday for good reasons," laughed Webster the gauger. "Now, Selkie, I'm taking this stuff to my house to keep until the cutter calls, and I want you and your yawl to transport it to Elsness."

"Me? No, no, Mr. Webster. You know what I was like before. I'll not touch the stuff again either in the barrel or in the glass. Get some poor body that needs the money. My wife and me will suffer if I do this."

"In the King's name, Mr. Ward. You and your wife do not matter. In the King's name!"

"You mean the . . ." Erchie stopped, recollecting his last attempt to correct the same exciseman.

"I mean His Majesty, William the Fourth, the King. This ignorant lad, Selkie, thinks Elizabeth is still Queen, and no doubt the *Skua* was Drake's *Golden Hind* anchored off Plymouth Hoe. Thank God there are going to be more schools. By the time your lads' sons are as old as these two are now, there will be schools for all."

He paused after voicing this generous thought, and Erchie wondered what the gauger would think if he told him the names of six successors to William IV, along with their histories.

"Now Selkie," Mr. Webster continued, "we'll go and tell that wife of yours it is in the King's name."

Selkie hesitated for a moment, and then said sadly, "Come with us, boys," and followed the gauger who was striding towards his cottage.

The gauger entered without ceremony, and immediately began, "Good-day, Mrs. Ward." Seawife put down the basket she was shaping, and removed the grass she was holding in her teeth. "I've ordered Selkie to come with his yawl and transport illicit cargo, to wit three kilderkins of rum and one firkin of brandy, from Quoyness to Elsness.

He will be well paid for it, but seems to think you will not like it."

Seawife's face fell. "Oh, Selkie," she exclaimed.

"Lass, lass," said Selkie, "you know it's not with me will that I touch the stuff."

"I vouch for that, good woman," added the gauger. "It's in the King's name. While we're looking after His Majesty's interests, you can teach these ignorant lads from the South the names of the monarchs since Elizabeth. They think she's still our Queen—though she never was of these lands."

Seawife looked at the two boys, and for a moment she brightened—one eyeball rolled, and she almost winked. But the concerned expression returned. "Me and the children will watch for thee comin' home, Selkie. What must be, must be." And she took up the grass and the basket.

Erchie and Mansie would have preferred to leave with the men, but they felt that Seawife would not like to see them interested in what was so distasteful to her. They stayed with the family, a family possessed by restlessness for the remainder of the day. Mathew and Mark, like their mother, had periods of listening intently and sniffing the air, of going to the window and staring out, and the younger children were fretful. The two boys felt the tension so much that they edged outside and wandered down to the geo. The *Kittiwake*, deep in the water, was standing out towards Elsness, Selkie at the helm, the gauger just in front of him, and Bob and Jeems far forward. They watched the yawl round Beaness and disappear into Kettletoft Bay.

"And there's no pier," mused Erchie.

"There's an old slip, Erch, at Elsness. It would have been built in the old days."

"In the old days? But we're in them, Mansie."

77

"Aye, so we are. We're out of the day after tomorrow and into the day afore yesterday."

"But how? How can it be?"

"It appalls me. We came here with the flood tide and full moon. Boy, I never saw an ebb like this."

Erchie was silent for a time, and then said, "Perhaps we got into this to clear up the mystery of our great-great-grandmother."

"Maybe. I don't know. Take things as they come, Erch."

They sat on the cliff top watching for the return of the *Kittiwake*, anxious to carry word to Seawife. But nothing appeared. The sun began to sink; not a thing on the sea. A small voice sounded beside them, and Mark was there, his big eyes troubled. "Mother says for you to come to suppèr." And he turned to his home. The boys followed him without a word.

The meal was a silent one until Erchie asked, "What will they do with those barrels? Pour the contents away?"

"That's what they should do, Erch," said Seawife. "But the gauger drinks, and so does Bob and so does Jeems. Selkie will be hard put to it."

The boys could find nothing more to say. The tension that held the family did not ease. Little ears and noses seemed to strain to the sea, seeking to get word of a returning father. Mansie and Erchie left after saying goodnight. They went down to the geo again in a waning moon. Nothing was to be seen in the dim light. Slowly they wandered back to the barn, and lay down in the hay. They turned and twisted, and at last slept uneasily.

Chapter 13

SELKIE'S RETURN

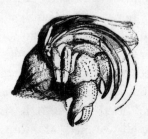

THE NEXT DAY STARTED as sadly and as silently as the afternoon of the day before. Feeling helpless to relieve the strain, Erchie suggested to Mansie at breakfast that they should go to Quoyness to see where the casks had been buried. They both looked to Seawife, seeking her approval. She did not speak at first, and they feared they had added to her sorrow, but she surprised them by saying, "We'll all come, but first we'll go to the pastures to see if the beasts are doing well." She put peerie Peter in her shawl, and they all trooped out. Erchie took little Andrew on his back, and Mansie was going to hoist Jeems up, but the little fellow put his hand in Mansie's and waddled along beside him. The two hoped that Seawife had rid herself of her fears for Selkie, fears that they could not understand.

The whole family went up the slope and into the small field of the sheep. The lambs came running to them, and the ewes followed slowly. Seawife and her boys went among them, she patting them with her free hand, her children fondling them, as did Mansie and Erchie. One little lamb put its fore-feet on Erchie's shoulder so that it could nose little Andrew's chubby hand. Slowly they went

79

to the stile into the field for the horses and cows, the sheep looking mournfully at them as they climbed over. Foal and calves trotted forward to be stroked. The horses and cows following more sedately. Each got its caress and all came with the family to the gate. After they had passed through, the two horses put their heads over to watch them, and the foal whinnied for them to come back.

Shortly after reaching the cliff's edge, Seawife stopped and faced Elsness, her face rapt. The boys saw the *Kittiwake* sailing along the Elsness land.

"There she is," cried Erchie. "Oh, she'll be back soon now." But as they all watched, Mansie was worried. "She should be changing direction," he muttered.

Both boys glanced at Seawife. Her expression had changed and saddened. She and her children stood perfectly still. The yawl sailed on until it reached the point and then rounded it and went out of sight. It was not coming home. The boys saw tears run down the faces of Seawife, Mathew, and Mark, while the others stared solemnly seaward.

"They must have heard of another smuggler," Erchie suggested hopefully.

Seawife did not answer, but started walking towards Quoyness, her children and the two boys with her. From time to time she stopped, listened, and sniffed seaward. Silently all ten came to the far end of Quoyness, and went down on the shore. Seawife sat on the shingle, gently rocking peerie Peter in her shawl, her family gathered at each side. The tears fell from her eyes. Mansie and Erchie did not know what to do. They wandered off and came to the holes where the casks had been buried—three fairly large holes and one smaller. They noted the flattened shingle over which the casks had been rolled down to the sea. They returned to Seawife and drew her attention to the holes, but she did not even look. She was staring at the sea.

"You think he'll drink again?" asked Mansie in a low voice.

Seawife didn't answer, and Erchie added, "I don't think he will. He told us on our first day here how he had prospered since you came to him."

Seawife wiped the tears from her eyes. "Erchie, boy, you don't know what a job he had to stop it. If he starts again, now with all the children in the house. . . ." She stopped, and the tears flowed again as she gently swayed peerie Peter in her shawl, her family still pressed around her.

Once more, unable to give comfort, Mansie and Erchie went down to the water's edge, leaving the disconsolate family huddled on the rocks.

"There's a hermit crab," said Erchie, pointing into a pool.

"Aye," said Mansie.

They went a little farther and then turned back. Suddenly they saw Seawife get up and gaze intently seaward.

Seals were hurrying from Elsness Holm towards Hacksness, plunging and rising for air.

"What's the matter with the seals?" asked Erchie.

"They've been hunted," answered Mansie.

"Aye," said Mathew. "They're running away and will be going to mother's brother. Are they not, Mother?"

"Aye, Mathew boy, they're fleeing to my brother. Don't call now, for they'll not be safe till they get to him. Come, children," she said, and went slowly up the beach, Andrew and Jeems clinging to her skirt, the others waddling after.

"Come, Andrew, I'll carry you, and Mansie will carry Jeems."

The little fellow looked at Erchie with his large, brown eyes, and clung more tightly to his mother. She was dragging her feet now, her head bent forward, tears trickling on to peerie Peter's face.

When at last they reached home, the two lads stayed by the barn, seeing they could not soften the grief of the family. Seawife and her boys went on to the cottage without a word. The cousins, not knowing what to do, drifted off, went down to the crags and looked into the geo.

"That's the old black dinghy Mrs. Dearness gave to Seawife, isn't it, Mansie?"

"Aye. And Selkie's creels a' lying high and dry for a good job. The wind's risin' and it's going to blow."

"A storm?"

"Like enough."

Erchie thought for a moment and said, "Do you think Seawife knew it was coming and feared for Selkie?"

"I doubt it, Erch. She would have said it if she did."

"The spray's dashing on the rocks now where we stood when that sailor shouted at us—after Selkie and you saving him."

"Aye, Erch, and Seawife, too, and I don't ken what's coming out of it."

"It seemed fine till the exciseman came."

"Aye. Seawife senses something. I don't know what."

Spray flying off the rocks blew towards the boys when they reached the geo, and the sea was dark and flecked with white caps. They turned back and, taking the same path up which they had supported Seawife seven days earlier, returned to the barn.

A low voice at their side startled them. "Mother says for you to come for something to eat," said Mark.

"Yes, Mark, but we're not hungry," said Erchie.

"Nor me neither, but Mother says we must eat."

The three went to the cottage and entered.

"We see no sign of the boat," said Erchie, "and the sea's rising."

"Nay, no boat," said Seawife, and set their supper in front of them. "Come children, and eat while I give peerie Peter his bottle."

They sat at the table, the little boys nibbling at their food, Mansie and Erchie almost choking at each bite. They sat for a long time, getting little food down. Suddenly a noise sounded above the wind. The children jumped from the table and gathered round their mother. Erchie and Mansie rose and faced the door.

The door was pushed open, and the gauger struggled in, supporting a helpless Selkie.

"It's all right, good wife," said the gauger loudly. "He's only drunk."

"Selkie!" she whispered, putting down the baby's bottle and holding the child with both arms.

"Now, woman, it's just a bit. Every man of us is the better for one now and then. I'll come back to pay him soon," and he settled Selkie in the armchair.

"There, Selkie, you're safe in your own house with your wife and children. Good-bye, good wife. I'll see that Lyall and Odie make the yawl safe in this wind."

Seawife did not answer, and the gauger went out.

Selkie mumbled incoherently in his chair.

Chapter 14

SEAWIFE DEPARTS

SELKIE ROLLED HIS EYES, focused them momentarily on his family, then looked down, tears running down his cheeks. The family, all except the baby, stared at him with large moist eyes. Erchie, feeling the strain, clutched Mansie's hand, and both turned away. Outside, the wind gusted around the stone house.

The strain was broken by peerie Peter who reached out his little arms to his father, saying something like "dee-dee." Selkie buried his face in his hands. When he looked up, his wife smiled wanly at him. She went over, put the child in his father's arms and a hand on his shoulder, her long hair falling about him as she did so.

"Oh, boy, could you not have got this summer past?"

"Lass! Lass! The smell o' brandy when they opened the cask, and the three o' them so hearty."

For a time no one spoke and no one moved. Then peerie Peter put his tiny hand up to his father's face. Selkie looked at him and uttered a broken sob.

Again a heavy approach sounded, and Jeems Lyall's bulk filled the doorway.

"Have ye not done enough bad for one day," snarled Seawife.

Lyall looked at her, his red face going a deeper red; then he spoke to Selkie.

"Thee boat, Ollie, is safely moored above the high tide mark. Bob's makin' her snug." Then he turned and faced Seawife. "And thee old boat, wife, will be in the sea if thoo does no look after it. And what's more, I forced no drink down thee man's throat." He strode to the door and went out.

Mansie said eagerly, "Erchie and me will go and make the dinghy safe."

He got no answer, and then just as he and Erchie were about to leave, Bob Odie entered, holding something under his arm. His yellow eyes flickered shiftily, and he scowled at the two lads. His high-pitched voice came fast.

"Here, Ollie, here's the hide o' the small thing you clubbed but would not skin. Being an honest neighbor, I'll not take it for myself. You might get a half-sovereign for it."

He flung something down, glanced around gloatingly, and went out into the gale.

The thing unfolded on the floor, fur down, blood-stained skin up. The two boys gasped. Seawife and her children were as motionless as the rocks on which seals rested. Selkie pressed the baby to his face to shut out the sight. Slowly his wife moved from him to her six sons and turned. They all stared at the skin.

"Oh, me Seawife," moaned Selkie. "Bitterly I repent. Oh, me children."

Seawife gave him a hard look and, her strong white teeth showing, snarled at him. "Peerie Peter can neither swim nor walk. He'll stay with ye. I also leave you that to remember me by." She pointed to the seal skin.

Selkie groaned as he rocked peerie Peter to and fro. Erchie could not stand it. "Oh, Seawife, don't go," he pleaded. "Look at the baby."

Seawife looked at the two boys, and so did her six sons. Her expression softened. "Sons o' Peter's sons, there's no blood between us. Tak' these to remember me by, ye wards o' the selkie folks."

She took the cord from her neck, and gave one amber bead to Erchie and the other to Mansie. "I'll no need them anymore," she said sadly.

The boys stared each at his own bead. Meanwhile Seawife picked up little Andrew. "Come children, home wi' me."

The seven passed out, their eyes filled with tears, without even glancing at Selkie. The door closed. The only sounds were those of the gusting wind and the labored gasps of Selkie. At last he spoke. "After her, boys. Bring her back to me and Peter!"

The boys put their beads into their jacket pockets and prepared to go.

"No, boys. No use. The curse o' Cain is on me," and he indicated the blood-stained sealskin.

Erchie and Mansie hesitated and watched Selkie clasping his youngest to his breast for a moment. He did not speak again. Mansie nudged Erchie. "We'll go after her," he whispered. "Come on."

The two went out into the black night and the howling wind.

Chapter 15

THE BLACK NIGHT

"DOWN TO THE SEA, ERCHIE. We must try and stop her."

As fast as they could in the darkness, Mansie and Erchie ran against the gale and came to the cliff edge. Just below them, Seawife was launching the old dinghy over the rocks by which the sea heaved and flowed. Down the path ran the two boys, and scrambled over the rocks to her side. Mathew was just getting in. The other five were already huddled in the stern of the boat.

"Seawife! Seawife!" they shouted.

She stood waiting, holding the boat by its painter, her clothes flapping around her, her hair blowing wildly in the wind.

"The dinghy can't live in that sea," panted Mansie.

"Nay, Mansie. Thee and Erchie must go back noo." She got in, put the oars in the rowlocks and started to pull away.

"Come back!" shouted Erchie. "There's nowhere for us to go now. Selkie told us to leave. There's no place to go!"

"Ye're goin' home too, boys, but not wi' me and me

children." The dinghy was rocking and plunging away and now passed outside the shelter of the geo. Now it rose against the waves then staggered into the troughs, driven swiftly across the bay and soon becoming blurred to a small black ball in the dark night. The boys scrambled along over the slippery rocks, trying to keep the blur in sight. On past Langigeo they hurried, Mansie hoping that the dinghy might be driven inshore at this point. But they could now see nothing.

"There she is!" shouted Mansie.

"Where? Yes—Oh!" Erchie slipped on the rock and fell, his leg bent under him.

Mansie, in his excitement did not notice and ran on. Erchie got up, able to walk, but his leg pained him.

"Come on, Erch, or we'll never see her again."

"Go on, Mansie. I can't keep up."

Erchie managed to keep Mansie in sight and followed him from the rocks on to Beasand where Mansie went more slowly, peering into the white-capped breakers that roared in. He stopped, and Erchie caught up with him, breathless.

"I've lost sight o' her altogether," he cried. "You're breathing over hard, Erch."

"I fell on the rocks and hurt my leg. It's sore, but not bad."

"I think we've lost her, but she could be driven in on this side o' Beaness."

They trudged over the sands to the old churchyard, ever stopping to peer into the seething waters. Past the burial place they went, this time with no thought of ghosts, and then along the edge of the sea.

"The wind's not so strong, Mansie."

"No. She might yet be safe. But where is she going?"

Erchie shook his head. Then he brightened. "Could it be to her brother?"

"I was wondering."

They felt weary now, but the gale was no longer lashing them. They stood searching—searching near in and then as far out as they could see. The waves no longer clipped white, and nothing helped to show up a black shape in the darkness.

"Queer how the wind died so quickly," muttered Mansie. "And there's fog all around, just after a gale."

"Mansie! A seal's head, isn't it?"

"Where? Aye. A pup. It must have lost its mother in the storm, poor thing. No, there's another, a big one."

"Look, Mansie. The boat!"

A dark object swirled past, missing the rocks, driven seaward. "The boat is upside down," cried Erchie.

Five more heads appeared around the boat, which was being carried rapidly out of sight. Then the heads disappeared.

"Seawife and her children," gasped Erchie.

"Best guess, Erch," murmured Mansie, staring on into the gloom. "The boat will go on past Elsness now. We'll not see it again."

For a long time they stared into the black waters, and seeing nothing, turned inland. They dragged their way up on the beach and, without thinking, came to the place where the pier should be.

"The fog's queer," said Mansie wearily.

"I suppose it is. It doesn't matter now."

"No pier. No village."

"Mansie, I could lie down and die."

"Erchie, boy. Is your leg sore?"

"It's stiff, but it's not that."

"No. Here's Towrie's Green again. We might as well sit down for a while. It's so black we can't see the house that was here when we landed."

They sat down, side by side, Erchie absent-mindedly rubbing his leg. There on the shingle, they peered into the dark sea, dejected and hopeless.

Chapter 16

THE FOG LIFTS

MANSIE STARTED. A shape appeared in the darkness. He watched it to make sure it was real. It loomed nearer, and Erchie now saw it. The dip of oars sounded faintly, and the drip of water between strokes.

"Her boat, Mansie," breathed Erchie.

They jumped up and ran down to the edge of the water.

"It looks too big, Erch, but the fog . . ."

A voice droned from the black boat. "Anybody want to go to the *Sigurd?*"

"Henry!" exclaimed both boys. "Yes, yes!"

The boat was wheeled around and backed in. The boys scrambled in over the stern, and immediately the oarsman pulled away. They huddled together on the tar coated timbers in the stern, as they had done before.

"Oh, thank you, Henry," said Erchie.

No answer came from the oarsman. There was only the rhythmic creak and splash of oars and the faint swish of the wash.

After a time, the familiar voice droned, "Ye'll find Henry bye and bye, bye and bye."

Before either boy could say anything, a series of joyful yelps sounded, and the bulk of the *Sigurd* loomed up in the fog.

"Here ye are," droned the voice as the boat drew alongside. "Climb aboard."

The boat rocked slightly as the boys reached up and climbed over the bulwarks to be greeted by the collie who nuzzled first one boy and then the other. The boat meanwhile faded to a blur as it was rowed away. A faint call sounded. Erchie leaned out over the railing. "Henry! Is Seawife with you?"

No answer came.

"Mighty, Erch. It must have been mother's brother."

"Seawife and her boys. Could they be with him?"

"Maybe, Erch. Maybe."

"Oh, she must be."

"But the capsized boat, Erchie. I don't think she can unless . . . Erch! The kelpies!"

"Oh, yes. There—they've gone."

They stared at the sea and then at each other.

"You were saying Seawife could not be with her brother unless . . . ?"

"Unless she is a wife from the sea, Erchie."

They stood pondering, the collie nosing them to claim attention.

Weariness after all their exertions now overcame them. They moved slowly up the companionway to the bridge deck and sat down. Their eyelids drooped, but they could not quite sleep. Erchie did doze off, to wake with a start thinking of the bodies of Seawife and her six sons dashed around by the sea. Both were dozing when a shout startled them.

"Up the both of you. Don't you see your folks waiting at the pier?"

It was the old sailor who had told them in fun not to lean against the fog.

The boys stood up, stiff and sore. It was broad daylight, the warm sun in the southwest.

"How long have we been here?" Erchie asked.

"Better than four hours," answered the sailor, and went to the bow.

Kettletoft village lay in the sunshine with pier, stores, houses, and Towrie's Green as they had known it. People stood on the pierhead waiting for the *Sigurd.* Erchie reached down and rubbed his leg.

"My leg was pressing against that stanchion," he said, as if an explanation were needed.

"Erchie boy, I've been seven days with Selkie Ward and his sea wife."

"So have I. It seemed like a dream."

"Aye. It must have been . . . but Erch!"

"What is it?"

Mansie was fiddling in his jacket pocket. He held out his open hand. "Seawife's!" An amber bead lay in the palm.

Erchie thrust his hand into his pocket and brought out another amber bead.

"She said she would not need them any more," said Erchie sadly.

After a pause Mansie muttered, "Aye, Erch. But *we* might."

The *Sigurd* drew alongside the pier and the passengers prepared to disembark.

GLOSSARY

ABOOT—about

AFORE—before

AROOND—around

AYE—yes

BENROOM—inner room of a small cottage

BLUE-JACKET—a sailor

BONNY—healthy, pleasant appearing, charming

BUITS—boots

DID NO—did not

DOON—down

EXCISEMAN—an official who inspects and rates articles to be taxed. He often collects payments of the tax.

GAUGER—exciseman who checks, measures, and determines the tax on goods like liquor

GEO—small inlet or gulley

HEADLAND—a point of high land jutting out into the sea

HOOSE—house

HOWE—a hollow or valley

KELPIE—Scottish name for a spirit that appears in the shape of a horse. The kelpies are said to haunt bodies of water and to enjoy the drowning of ship travelers.

KEN—to know, to perceive

LAIRD—owner of a small estate

MALT—grain like barley and oats steeped in water, often ground for use in brewing

NOO—now

OGT—out

PEERIE—small

QUAY—a wharf

THEE—your

THOO—you

WHIT—what

WI'—with

YE—you

NAUTICAL TERMS

AFT—near the stern or rear of a boat or ship

BOW—the forward of a boat or ship

BOWSPRIT—a strong spar or boom projecting forward from the bow of a vessel

DINGHY—small light rowboat

GUNWHALE—upper edge of boat's or ship's side

HALYARD—rope or tackle for hoisting and lowering (as a yard, spar, sail, flag)

JIB—three-cornered sail that extends forward from the foremast of a boat

JIBE—to shift suddenly from one side to another, as a sail under certain conditions

MAST—long pole that rises into the air from the bottom of a boat that supports the sails and rigging

PAINTER—rope attached to the bow of a boat, used for tying the boat to a pier

PORTSIDE—the left side of the ship, facing forward

REEF—to reduce the area of a sail by rolling or folding a portion at the head or foot and securing to the spar

SLOOP—a sailing vessel with one mast and a fore-and-aft mainsail and jib

SPAR—long, rounded piece of wood to which a sail is fastened

STANCHION—an upright bar, post, or support

STERN—the rear end of a boat or ship

TACK—to change the direction of a ship

THWART—a rower's crosswise seat in a boat

TO WINDWARD—in the direction from which the wind blows

YARD—a long spar used for supporting a sail, especially any of the sails of a square-rigged vessel

YAWL—2-masted sailboat with the shorter mast aft of the point at which the stern enters the water